Empress
Of All The Stars
A Novel of the
Empyrean Republic

By Matt Kirkby

1 Chapter One

"It's a trap!"

"Do you think so?" Devin couldn't help but make the comment even though he was alone in the cockpit of his aerospace fighter. The region of space around Stella's Folly had been a fierce battleground for the last twenty minutes. Warships loyal to House Simard had reached the comet first and sprung a perfect trap on the unwary brigantine that House LaLonde had sent to claim the comet for its own use. A *Sheathe*-class brigantine and its full complement of *Stilettos*, plus a *Broadsword* and its own fighter squadron had sprung out of the comet's tail and attacked Garnet Flight before the *Reliance* could respond.

The com-system crackled with static before clearing into a tension-filled voice. *"Fighter Group, there's a new group of signals appearing on our main scopes. Enemy reinforcements are approaching."*

"Thanks for the head's up!" Devin Shaw cursed under his breath as his fightercraft's sensors screamed out warnings about multiple enemy targeting locks. "Too little, guys, too late." Pulling sharply on the throttle, he triggered the thrusters and flipped his *Stiletto* end-over-end so that it was facing back in the direction it just come from.

Momentum of course, still carried the *Stiletto* along its previous vector and at its previous speed so Devin was actually flying backwards, still pursued by three enemy *Stilettos*.

"You won't get me so easily." Devin triggered all of his starfighter's weaponry with a press of the firing stud. The twin laser beams missed the lead enemy starfighter, but its two companions broke away from their formation as the *adder*-class missiles streaked towards them. Devin flipped his fighter end-over-end again and accelerated away along a new vector before the Simards could regroup. He cleared his throat. "Emerald Group," he said loud enough to trigger the com-system, "report in."

"Emerald Two, still here."

"Emerald Four, kicking ass and taking names."

"Emerald Eight, can we go home yet?"

"Emerald Nine here. The techs are gonna kill me when they see this fighter's armor."

Devin sighed. *Too many losses,* he thought grimly. *We're not going to win this one.* He reached for the comm-controls to manually change the radio frequencies. *"Reliance,* this is Emerald Leader. Requesting orders."

"Emerald Leader, break off the engagement," the voice of the brigantine's comm-officer crackled back to him through static. Both sides routinely attempted to jam each other's transmissions as common battlefield practice; winning the electronic battlefield could be more important than the actual fighter combat. *"Return to base. We're withdrawing. That is a priority one order."*

"Understood, *Reliance."* Devin changed frequencies again. "All Emeralds, return to the ship. Priority one command." He tried to clear his sensor screen, but debris from the comet's tail was confusing his sensors. *Which readings are from ships and which are just chunks of rock and ice?* He was still wondering when a *Broadsword* painted blue-with-yellow-trim emerged from behind a spray of icy shards almost close enough for him to each out and touch. "Simard *Broadsword* coming out of the tail!" he warned over the comm. He tried to erase the panic from his voice. *Fat chance of that happening.* "Simard *Broadsword* is closing." He accelerated away from the big warship. *I'm no match for that monster,* he told himself grimly. *Attacking it alone would be suicide.* It was a bitter truth to swallow.

The newly arrived *Broadsword* launched its fresh fighter squadron, then began to move towards the beleaguered *Reliance.*

"Emerald Four here, is this a private parade or can anyone join?" The rest of Emerald flight's survivors fell into formation around Devin's fighter.

"This is no time for jokes," Devin replied coldly.

"Running away are we?"

"We don't have much choice." Devin could hear the bitterness in his voice, but didn't have the energy to mask it.

"The five of us won't be able to do much to the Broadsword.*"*

"Not unless we ram it."

"I want to live past today's battle, Four."

"Your loss, Eight."

"Cut the chatter, Flight." The *Reliance* was ahead of him. The red-and-green painted brigantine was battered, its once-gleaming hull now blackened by laser beams and missile impacts. Half of the ship's laser cannons were no longer firing, and only two or three of the point defense guns were fending off strafing runs by nearly a dozen Simard *Stilettos*. The fighters launched *adder*-class missiles and point defense hastily engaged them, allowing the fighters to regroup for another run.

"Hit them hard!" Devin ordered. He and the other surviving Emeralds tore through the Simard fighters, scattering most of them and leaving three enemy fighters as expanding clouds of debris.

Covered by the tattered remains of Emerald Flight, the *Reliance* turned and accelerated away from the comet.

The Simards did not pursue.

1 Chapter Two

"Flight Commander Shaw. Would you perhaps care to elaborate upon your earlier disposition?" The question was asked in a polite, cultured tone of voice by an elderly man who was dressed in a black business suit. His green-and-red striped tie showed his House allegiance, but even those colors were the darkest shades possible.

Devin remained sitting quietly at the small table across the narrow room from the civilian. "Yes, Inquisitor." He refrained from nervously smoothing non-existent wrinkles from his tunic. He was dressed in his best uniform, dark green with red stripes along his arms and legs, but felt uncomfortable. Nearly a month had passed since the battle, but he still felt tense. *Too much time on the flight back to Cadixia,* he thought. *Too many empty bunks in the flight decks.* Lost comrades could not be replaced until the *Reliance* had returned to one of the LaLonde holdings, in this case, the capitol. *Then coming home to the biggest city in the Freehold and being confined to base pending this damn fool hearing. The city is out there, and I'm stuck in here.*

Dominique Richesse, Lord Inquisitor of House LaLonde, leaned back in his chair. "Then feel free to proceed with your story." His blue eyes were sharp, but sunken into a face devoid of spare flesh...giving him an ominous skull-like appearance. "I am always interested in hearing from those involved in any incident."

"The battle of Stella's Folly was an ambush, pure and simple."

Richesse said nothing.

"Our advance patrol was jumped by superior numbers and caught completely off-guard. We attempted to fight the Simards, but were unable to gain any significant advantage." *We were totally out-gunned. We never stood a chance.* "Captain Massel had no choice but to withdraw his command from the comet's vicinity or else witness its utter destruction."

"The facts, Flight Commander, speak for themselves." Richesse waved a skeletal hand towards his computer monitor on which data flowed across the flat screen in steady streams. "Captain Massel failed to secure Stella's Folly for this House. He led his command into a textbook-basic ambush. He failed to inflict significant losses onto the enemy, despite taking severe losses to both of his own fighter squadrons and serious hull damage to his vessel. Aside from the fourteen pilots who were killed, he left five more pilots to the enemy."

"Massel had no choice!"

"So *you* claim."

Devin glared at the smug civilian. *How can you just sit there and pass judgment?* he thought. *You weren't there! You've probably never been near a battlefield yourself.* Inquisitors were political appointees, not trained soldiers. "Garnet Flight was patrolling ahead of us as we approached the Folly." With an effort, he forced his tone to remain calm and non-argumentative. "They were moving towards the comet in prelude to our sending over a research team to examine the comet." *We were hoping for a water-rich comet we could mine.* "The Simard ships emerged from the comet's tail and opened fire. A volley of *Adder*-class missiles destroyed half of Garnet before we even knew they were under attack. Emerald was scrambled and launched as quickly as we could get into our cockpits but Garnet was totally gone before we arrived. Emerald did what it could, but we were totally outnumbered and outgunned."

"House Simard fielded two *Broadswords* and a *Sheathe* against you."

Devin nodded. "Against the *Reliance*." *Against a lone Sheathe,* he thought to himself. "Simard had more than twice the fighters we had available, and their cruisers could have vaporized our lone brigantine. We inflicted what losses we could on them, but we never really stood a chance." He let his voice trail into silence.

The moment of silence stretched out.

Devin wished that he something to look at, but the conference room was depressingly barren. The uncomfortable chair in which he sat at the plain wooden table—plain unpolished pine, he thought. A single glass of untouched water, now sweating in the corner. The austere wooden table and chair at which the Inquisitor studied his computer monitor. Beige walls, slate-colored tiles on the floor. A cold room. *Not a place anyone would feel comfortable in. No, not a welcoming room at all.* A thought struck him. *Not even a banner in our House colors!* He noted that with surprise. *A bland room which could belong to any House.*

Richesse seemed unmoved by the story, or the long silence. "The comet was a valuable prize, Flight Commander. It could have been exploited to supply our colony on Miser with potable water. Instead, we shall have to divert civilian freighters and appropriate escorts to transport water there from our holdings on Sapphire."

Devin sighed aloud as he acknowledged the political realities of that assignment. "Which will affect the war effort."

"*Everything* affects the war effort." Richesse leaned back in his chair with an arrogant smirk on his face. He tapped his fingers against each other in a slow rhythm. "The Noble Houses have been fighting for dominance since Landfall. The struggle will not end until one House or another becomes supreme over the Cadian People." His voice held no uncertainty of which House he wished to see become the dominant power.

"The Resource Wars have drained our culture," Devin protested almost without thinking. "Centuries of constant warfare with no clear victor. All we have left is chaos. There's no point to it."

The Inquisitor's eyes narrowed. "Such talk could be considered treasonous."

Devin snorted. "I thought that House LaLonde encouraged its officers to think for themselves."

"Within reason."

"If we don't think for ourselves, then we might as well belong to Thibeau or Chenier."

"House LaLonde has guided its holdings well for centuries. There are far worse Houses to belong too. Houses where a failure of this extent in battle would have been punished far more severely than receiving a mere reprimand on your record."

"Is this nonsense over then?"

"Yes." The Inquisitor examined his computer. "You are dismissed, Flight Commander."

1 Chapter Three

Lord Nicholaus Karul paced along his favorite balcony in his family's manor house. He had a beautiful view of the heavily forested countryside, which he normally found soothing. *Today, I can take little solace in the forest,* he thought sadly. *The press of duty weighs heavily upon my shoulders.* "Why do I constantly find myself at the mercy of fools?" he demanded aloud. "That comet could have been a valuable prize for our House and you allowed the Simards to gain control of it."

"We did our best, Lord." The captain watched his Lord pacing along the balcony with a faint hint of concern. "The Simards arrived first at the Folly and fought off a LaLonde patrol with minimal losses. We lacked the strength to then seize it from them."

"Lacked the *strength*, Captain, or lacked a warrior's courage?"

"I live to serve this House. My courage and my honor are intact."

"Do you really serve this House, Shettel?"

The officer saluted, one hand against his heart. "My life is yours, Lord Karul." Karul was a fair man, never punishing his subordinates for failures beyond their control. He squared his shoulders, the gold trim on his slate-gray uniform glinting in the sunlight.

"Never forget that fact." With a resigned sigh, Karul turned back to the view of the forest. "Leave me. Prepare my shuttle and a small escort. I must travel to Arcadion for the next Conclave."

"Yes, my Lord. The shuttle, and your escort, will be ready to depart within the hour." He turned and strode back into the building.

"The next Conclave," Karul muttered after Shettel had vanished into the office. "Which will be like all of the previous ones and likely all those yet to come. Seemingly endless chatter from the mush minds who govern the other Noble Houses. Threats and taunts and bickering which ultimately come to no resolution." The annual Conclaves were a complete waste of time and energy. "Unless one can change them." He chewed at his inner lip as he considered that particular thought. "If one House becomes dominant, then *everything* changes."

Now that was a risk worthy of taking.

* * *

"Closing on ACG-Delta-Two."

"Launch our fighters. Order them to make a clean sweep of that sector." Martin Reeve eyed the tactical display with a careful eye. "Engage at will."

"Confirmed."

Martin waited as his patrol made its careful advance. One *Sheath*-class brigantine and three cruisers, with half a dozen freighters, slowly advancing into an asteroid cluster controlled by House Graham. *The possibilities for success or failure are right within my grasp...a glorious time to be alive.* His name would be recorded within the House Archives for this day's mission. *I just hope it gets recorded as a glorious victor and not a failure colored forever with the stain of defeat.* "Scan for power emissions." Which asteroid should he concentrate on? There were so many in the area.

"Scanning."

"Fighters launched. Taking up defensive formation around us."

"No sign of enemy fighters yet?"

"Nothing on our scopes, Captain."

"Keep scanning." Surely the locals *must* have spotted his fleet by now? *Can their security be this lax?* he wondered. *No Bouchard commander would leave a facility vulnerable.* Any scan-tech who failed to detect an enemy fleet had better hope to die in battle before facing the punishment Bouchard would devise.

Soft chatter between the bridge stations kept the mood tense. Martin forced himself to stand by the main display—though he desperately wanted to pace and wear away some of his nervous energy. *That would not be the image I need to project,* he reminded himself. *The eyes of my Lord are upon me this day. I must not disappoint him.* Honor could accept no less. Instead, he gave a quick study of his uniform. The indigo of his uniform was offset by thin sage piping and his medals and pins of rank were recently polished.

"Captain, two freighters have been detected in orbit of asteroid designated delta-five-seven. Power emissions are in stand-by modes. Hard to see them, but they're there."

"We must have eluded the Graham patrols then." Martin smiled with mingled relief and feral anticipation after the report was completed. "Lord Bouchard *will* be pleased." A costly battle against alert defenders would earn him no favor in his Lord's eyes—it was far better to score a victory with the minimal expenditures of House resources. "Order the *Stilettos* to strafe the freighters and then accept their surrender." The freighters would not be able to offer much of a fight. On a battlefield, they were just big targets. "Prep the shuttles for launch. I want our marines on the ground *now*!" His *Sheathe* carried one hundred and seventy-five marines; each cruiser in his convoy carried forty more. "Secure those mines at any cost."

"Yes, Sir."

Securing the mines would be easy. The real challenge—and the risk—would come in getting his marines from the warships to the surface. *We just have to take the shuttle pads first, then secure the colony's command center. Once there, we will have complete control of the life support systems. If the Grahams resist, then we destroy their life support and let their workers slowly suffocate in those tunnels.* Not that it would come to that. After centuries of inter-House warfare, such mass destruction was unnecessary. *Graham will yield to us easily enough. They will just plot to retake the asteroid cluster in a future battle.* Such was the nature of life in the Cadixian Freeholds.

* * *

Baxter's was a busy bar, crowded with drinkers representing just about every House and faction. Although it was located in Karul neighborhood, it drew its clientele from every House. Mostly soldiers, with some traders and a handful of ordinary laborers.

Devin was slumped against one of the tables near the back of the main room. There were half a dozen alcoves spaced around the main room, but they had already been occupied when he had first arrived several hours before.

"Doing your best to subsidize the bar, Flight Commander?"

"Hey, Jennifer," he slurred. "Have a drink."

"No, thank you." She looked at her commanding officer with something close to disgust. "I would have expected better from you." Her veridian jumpsuit looked very military.

Devin sighed. *Same old mother hen she always is*, he thought. "What else is there to while on leave?" he demanded, pushing himself into a more upright sitting position. "It's not like anyone wants to associate with us." Defeat had a stench that kept other personnel far away.

"We need to keep in training. We could get reassigned at any moment."

"Jennifer, you are so naïve."

"Better to be naïve then whatever you are. Sir," she added after too long a pause.

Devin eyed her for a long moment.

She looked back at him with that quiet contempt.

"Well what do we have here?"

Devin turned his head to the left and looked up at owner of that smirking voice. The man looked as if he had been poured into his form-fitting blue uniform. The saffron trim showed his House affiliations clearly. *He's kinda cute, but for that one small fact.* "A Simard rat."

The man shook his head in amusement. "Better Simard than LaLonde. Better a manure shoveler than a LaLonde."

Devin's glass shattered on the floor as his fist connected with the Simard's officer's face.

1 Chapter Four

"Warfare is costly." Jacques Simard stared at the budget report with bleary eyes. "Five million credits apiece for a *Sheathe*-class brigantine. Two million and forty thousand credits for a *Broadsword* cruiser."

"Plus the cost of training the crew."

"Plus two hundred thousand credits apiece per *Stiletto* fighter." Twenty-four of which could be berthed on a *Sheathe* and twelve on a *Broadsword*. "Outfitting a military fleet grows ever more expensive."

"Makes a *Mule*-class freighter a bargain at six hundred and fifty thousand credits, yes?" Roy Simard chuckled as he set his own hardcopy report onto the desktop. He was wearing a working uniform, with its lemon-colored sleeves puffed out at the shoulders and coming to tight cuffs at his wrists. His indigo pants were snug and tucked into knee-high brown boots. "Nineteen thousand metric tons of cargo is cheap."

Jacques shook his head. "I know all this." His own uniform was wrinkled, though cut in the same fashion and colors.

"But you still need to review the files. Record-keeping, boring as it is, remains vital to the smooth functioning of our economies." Roy kept his voice calm, though privately he shared the other man's boredom. He reached for one of the water glasses, leaving behind a water ring on the carved oak of the tabletop. "We need to maintain a large number of commercial freighters to carry resources from the asteroids to our refineries and factories. We can hardly afford to strip-mine Cadixia." As the only life-bearing world in the system, Cadixia was a vital to the continued survival of the Cadian People.

"Our Freeholds are not the independent states we like to think they are. We all rely on supply transports to maintain our colonies and outposts. We need a constant flow of resources to keep the far-flung factories in operation and then to carry completed goods to the waiting markets." Markets both within the parent Freehold and amongst the holdings of the other Houses. "Those freighters are the weakest links in our defenses." Jacques rubbed at his eyes, then winced as his hand brushed against the bruise on his cheek.

"Indeed. Now you see why we need a steady supply of warships."

"Which costs us resources we obtain from the asteroids...thus requiring more freighters to mine the asteroids and thus more warships to protect them. It seems to be a vicious circle."

"Comments like those, Jacques lead me to think that you are wasted on that *Sheathe*. You could have a steady job here."

"I'm not cut out to be part of the Admiralty. I like to command my own ship." To be far away from convoluted family politics and inter-House squabbles was a more truthful explanation. "I like having clearly defined enemies. Simple decisions."

"Life or death decisions?"

"I have to make them when they're presented...and I live or die with the results of my choice." Warfare was much cleaner than politics.

Roy Simard shook his head. "You need to grow up sometime, Jacques. You can't deny your family responsibilities forever."

Jacques sighed.

Incorrigible. Roy shook his head. "You need to stay out of those bar brawls. They are most unbecoming for an officer in a House Navy. Let alone a scion of said House."

"You should see the other guy," Jacques protested.

Roy chuckled.

"Can we take a break?"

"A short one." Roy dropped the stack of hardcopy onto the tabletop and followed his nephew into the corridor. "All those numbers are making my eyes ache."

"Mine were aching before I started reading."

"I've warned you about those bars."

Jacques nodded his head in resignation. "I know, I know. No place for a scion of a Noble House, et cetera." He pushed through the doorway onto a small rooftop patio. And blinked in the wan sunlight.

Despite the clouds obscuring the spring-time sun, the city of Cadixion was a beautiful place. Buildings rose gracefully to dizzying heights. Banners flapped atop many of them, proclaiming territorial boundaries. Parks made pools of green, and the blue of canals crisscrossed the city.

"A nice view."

"Hardly seems appropriate to have a military base in the heart of a city."

Roy chuckled. "And what would you say to a world which has a dozen such bases within its capitol?"

"I would think the inhabitants were mad." Jacques shook his head. The city was divided amongst the Noble Houses and each House maintained a sizable military garrison, even though the planet was supposed to be neutral ground. "The Resource Wars touch even here," he grumbled. "We should not have to maintain weapons here. This world should remain pure."

"Sometimes I doubt Humans can maintain the purity of anything." Roy took a drink from the water cup in his hand.

"We're doomed to war?"

"We are caught within the demands of honor and politics. I often think that the two are mutually exclusive."

A bulky shuttle dropped through the low-lying clouds towards the space port on the outskirts of the city.

"All we can hope to do is protect our holdings and trust that the other Houses will continue to respect the neutrality and sanctity of Cadixia."

"And if not?"

"Then," his uncle replied in a cold voice, "the Freeholds as we know them, are doomed."

* * *

Marc LeMat eyed the bulky shuttle as it landed on the pad amid a plume of exhaust gases. "That's the fourth *Packrat* to land today."

"Yep." Ian Keating kept his voice calm as he hastily pulled a computer-pad from inside one of the pockets in his ivory jumpsuit. He keyed the pad on and waited for the screen to brighten.

The Port Control Officer turned to look at Ian. "Isn't it unusual for this many *Packrats* to land in one day?"

"Lady Thibeau is shipping in a lot of new equipment." He checked the manifest before handing it over to the other officer. "Everything is accounted for."

The gray-uniformed man flipped through the electronic pages in a distracted manner. "Agricultural equipment? Computer cores. Standard environment prefab construction kits. What is she building?"

"We're upgrading some of our facilities on Leroux Isle," Ian told him in a bored voice. "I'm not even really needed here." He chuckled softly as Marc glanced at the sidearm holstered to his waist. "Who is going to try and steal agricultural equipment?"

"Not many I dare think." The PCO laughed. "Not much call for such things."

"Nope. Just for expanding some of our farming facilities."

"Good luck with that."

Ian nodded in genuine thanks. *Nice to be reminded that not every inter-House interaction involves the exchange of firepower.* "We're only landing here because Leroux isn't equipped to handle *Packrats*."

"So you'll have to transship them?"

"Surface ocean freighter I think is the plan. Cheaper than sending out dozens of *Handlers*."

"No doubt."

"I'm just glad I don't have to be the one overseeing the details for this expansion."

"You and me both."

"I just have to see the *Packrats* unloaded and then someone else can deal with the rest of the shipment."

"Good luck to you at least." The PCO offered the manifest back to Ian. "Everything looks to be in order. Have a good day."

"You as well."

1 Chapter Five

The Cadian House of Lords was situated in roughly the center of the largest continent on Cadixia, at the very heart of the capitol city. The main structure was a huge dome, surrounded by concentric rings of several dozen towers. Each Noble House had its own tower—the more powerful the House, the larger and more ornate its tower tended to be. A few towers stood ramshackle and long-deserted—testaments to Houses which had fallen from glory and into the obscurity of defeat.

The Grand Council Chamber was located, of course, in the tallest tower. It was a large, circular room with stone walls and a tiled floor. Banners hung along the wall, each bearing the colors and emblem of one of the Houses. A table with half a dozen chairs had been placed in front of each banner. Light came from ornate torches—neon bulbs worked to look like actual flames—on the walls and gave the assembled nobles wavering shadows

In small groups, men and women entered the chamber through the main doors. They tended to gravitate in small parties, giving the other groups a wide berth. The chief nobles of each House, along with a handful of advisors and aides. The Nobles wore the brightest hues, as befitted their importance, while their aides wore lesser shades of their respective House colors. Several dozen men and women in total had already assembled when Karul and his own entourage entered. He gave a few polite nods to the Nobles he actually liked, and a cold glare to the others. Aside from the colors of their respective Houses, the Nobles dressed in similar fashions—the men in tunics, snug pants, and half-capes; the women in floor-sweeping dresses—though the fabrics tended to vary in cut and quality.

An ornate clock chimed softly. The wood paneling of its case was carved with intricate care into swirls and fanciful shapes. The face was marked with the emblems of the various Houses, as well as the time.

"Lords of the Freeholds, I bid you welcome." Jonathan LaLonde eyed the others as they murmured their own greetings back. The Cadian Freeholds claimed one star system with eleven planets and forty or so moons. The Lords maintained holdings on four planets, eighteen moons, and countless sites amongst the asteroid belt. *So far I have some of the richest holdings, giving me power to call the session to order, if not enough to rule the entire system. Yet.* He adjusted the way his vermilion cloak fell over the shoulders of his carmine tunic. "Let this Conclave stand in session." His blue eyes drifted across the other Lords and towards Nicholaus Karul. *I am rich, yet* his *House maintains control over Bijou and its ruby mines.* The exquisite rubies were vital for the construction of laser weapons—being used to focus and amplify the beams of coherent light on warships. *Someday that ownership will change.* "May I be the first to offer sympathies to Lady Thibeau on the illness of her father."

Yvonne Thibeau nodded once. "Thank you, Lord LaLonde." She wore ivory robes, with a rich pomegranate cloak. White fur lined the edges of her cloak and silver chains hung from her neck. A gold locket hung between her breasts. Her hair was tied back in a complicated bun.

"I trust that your father will again take his place amongst us."

"Perhaps he will, Lord LaLonde. The favor of the universe will decide."

Bianca Tremblay gestured for attention. Her green cloak flapped like a bird's wings as she waved her slender arms. "I feel that we should begin more earnest talks in seeking peace. These endless wars are draining our culture. We all know this...why can't we admit it?"

"Because we are too obsessed with pride and honor," Jean-Paul Bouchard replied. "What House among us would be the first to surrender its sovereignty to another?" He had dispensed with his cape, standing in a plain indigo tunic and pants.

"None." Max Tessier was the first to reply. In his mostly gray tunic, he stood out against the colorful other Houses. "I will not yield

Maraselle to any other House...and I doubt any of you would cede territory to me."

Nicholaus Karul snorted aloud. "And this is the same reasoning that has kept our people at war for millennia. We should have out-grown this pettiness long ago. Before the Exile." His ebony tunic and pants were embroidered with gold trim.

"But we did not," Yvonne Thibeau pointed out. "We have all fought against each other since the dawn of time and will likely do so until one House finally rises to dominance over all others." And she knew just the House she wished to see dominant over all others. "Until that day comes, the Freeholds will only know war."

"War is an ugly term," Marcel Chernier commented. His maroon and silver clothing made a bold statement, though the rest of his entourage wore similar hues and he all but blended into their ranks. "The cycles of combat between our Houses merely serve to provide a controlled outlet for aggression. Our warriors gain honor from these limited battles."

"A controlled outlet?"

"Of course. We hardly condone our warriors to engage in indiscriminate slaughter. Battles are fought between warriors. Battlefields are best limited to the desolation of space."

"Or the conquest of mining colonies." Lord Graham glared at Bouchard as he made that comment

Bouchard took no notice of the glare.

"The destruction of cities and the slaughter of civilians do not occur," Chenier continued. "We limit the destructiveness of warfare and keep it away from the prizes we seek to control." He brushed at his thick brown beard.

"It remains a simple matter of might making right." Yvonne waved a slender hand. "The strong must dominate the weak. There can be no other means of maintaining order."

"We make war a legal tool of statecraft then?"

"Perhaps, Lord Karul, we have always done so."

"We merely follow the traditions of our ancestors," Yvonne pointed out. "They fought amongst each other for dominance and control over Arcadia's resources for millennia."

"I do not dispute that fact," Biannca announced after a moment, "though I wonder at the accuracy of our legends. Surely our ancestors could not have fought with such violence."

"You refer to the unification wars?"

"I refer to the legends which talk about entire cities being obliterated by *atomics*."

"That is barbaric," Lord Simard commented into the ensuing silence. "No true Cadian would condone such dishonorable tactics."

"Victory is the greatest honor."

"Not when it comes at such a price."

"You would sooner surrender then fight?"

"I would sooner surrender a city, even a world, then see it utterly destroyed by atomics."

"We have no atomics," Lord Karul reminded them. "Those weapons were lost during the Exile." *Thankfully*, he thought silently. *I would trust no House with the casual power to so easily destroy a city. One bomb and thousands would be dead. Where would such a battle end? How few survivors would there be?*

"And a good thing too."

"Indeed. If we had possessed such devices, they would have been used in some battle or other...entire worlds could have been left lifeless."

"No one would be that foolish, Simard."

"Are you so certain, Thibeau?"

"I am."

"Fah!"

"My House would not have sullied its honor by the indiscriminate destruction of a habitable world. Without Cadixia, we would all be dead."

"We have the colonial holdings."

"They are not enough to maintain us."

"They suffice."

"We need the openness of Cadixia to survive. We cannot hope to prosper if this world was to be rendered lifeless."

"So you say."

"Talk is cheap, Bouchard. Planets are not."

"Nor are warships. Take care lest your fleet becomes so much scrap."

Karul shook his head. *This bickering is pointless.* He banged his fist onto the table top, bringing the room into silence. "Let us start from a civil viewpoint." He paused a moment, waiting for the other Lords to settle themselves. "The ongoing clashes of our Houses stem from the division of natural resources."

"I do not argue that fact."

"Nor do any of us," Yvonne said.

"If a single strong central government was formed, the abundant natural resources of this system could be fairly divided amongst our people. We would know peace."

Bouchard snorted. "We have never known peace. It is an elusive concept."

"So you would prefer to see endless war?"

"I would prefer to see one House rule and the others disbanded, but that is bloody unlikely." Tessier chuckled. "And thus we come full circle to the futility of these Conclaves. We meet here and talk and talk and talk. We resolve nothing. We part company and issue new orders to our soldiers. The Resource Wars will continue."

"Until our society collapses?" Karul asked.

"Is it in any danger of collapse?"

"Do you think that we can continue to go on like this forever? Year after year of warfare...century after century of destruction and meaningless death?"

"I think you overreact." Biannca smiled. "Perhaps, if you feel that your holdings are on the verge of collapse, that you should consider joining with another House. I'm confident that any of us would be more than willing to assume administration over your holdings."

Karul sent her a glare. "My holdings are my own to administer."

"Thus, it goes," Tessier commented. "No alliance and thus no end to the cycle of violence."

1 Chapter Six

"It has been a long struggle, my Lady."

Yvonne Thibeau smiled and handed Chenier a jewel-encrusted goblet. "But perhaps the struggle will soon pay off."

Lord Marcel Chenier sipped his wine. "You have some advantage?" The emerald on his finger glinted in the light pouring through the windows of the suite.

"Let us say that history can be a fine teacher." She glided across the lush carpet of her private quarters. The folds of her snow-white dress flowed with her, a subtle illusion of slenderness and beauty. Her hair was, as usual, coiffed into an ornate design, with a hairnet inlaid with sparkling rubies. The white of her dress gleamed in the sunlight pouring through the windows.

Marcel was dressed in a simple tunic and pants, having dispensed with the half-cape. He wore his House colors proudly. A dark red tunic, almost a merlot, with silver stripes on the puffy sleeves matched the dark gray pants. His boots were polished so well that he could see his reflection in them—and count the gray hairs in his beard. "We know much of history, Yvonne. Every Cadian knows the Pre-Exile and Post-Landfall history of our people." He shrugged. "Our ancestors were once powerful nobles on Arcadia. Until the First Prince sought to join our world with some upstart interplanetary republic." *What had he been thinking?*

"The Republic was growing and its steady expansion through space brought them to our world and its colonies...what choice did they offer the First Prince?" she countered. "Those events are now so far removed that we know little of their outcome. After more than a thousand years, does the Republic even still exist? We *have* lost contact with them after all."

"Very true, Yvonne."

She paced through the room, her already-soft footsteps muffled by the thick turquoise carpet. "All that we know of the Republic is what our family histories recorded as happening at the time." *And not every family history agrees on the chain of events or their outcome. The bias to* elevate one's own House above all others was paramount among them all.

"The histories tend to agree on the main points," Marcel told her.

She looked at him more closely. *Reading my thoughts, eh Marcel?* "True. Many of our Houses refused to support the Prince's efforts. As the Republic fought battles to unify its member worlds and extend its control over the so-called civilized systems, our ancestors fought with the Prince's supporters over Arcadia's membership in the growing Republic."

"A pity that our ancestors lost that struggle."

"Indeed." *That is where my House began to lose its influence. Such a long decline...*

"It all went badly after the fighting began spreading to Arcadia's off-world colonies." Supposedly attacks against neutral shipping had finally brought the Republic officially into the civil war. *Just whom was sponsoring those attacks has been lost to history...if our ancestors ever knew it. Perhaps one of the so-called Rogue Houses, or maybe one of the Prince's supporters. Perhaps the Republic itself sought some pretext to invade...or maybe some real pirate group stumbled into the region and set up operations. If it was the last, then the universe does have a perverse sense of humor.* "If the Republic had not backed the Royal House with its off-world military units, then we would not have been exiled."

"Indeed not. One of *our* Houses might have become the Royal House."

"Indeed." She sighed at the lost chances. *Why didn't my ancestors seize the throne?* Surely the histories had exaggerated the unified strength of the Houses loyal to the Saint-Jamis family?

"Instead, we left Arcadia." Some family histories told of the Cadian Lords proudly choosing to leave Arcadia rather than submit to the rule of House Saint-Jamis and the Republic. Others told of families being herded onto waiting freighters at gunpoint. "We gave up our world to wander the stars."

"The Exile was a shaping for our people. It weeded out the weak Houses and made the rest of us stronger." Half a dozen of the former Great Houses had perished during the Exile. *The weak were purged or else absorbed into stronger Houses. Such is the way of things.* "The Exile led us to this world." Lady Thibeau finished her thoughts. "Cadixia has become a stronghold of power. We rival our ancestors in terms of honorable pursuits and cultural advancements."

His eyes flicked across the statues and other artwork which occupied the room. *It's so like Yvonne to hold a meeting to decide the future inside a museum dedicated to the past.* "Despite our Freeholds being confined within a single star system," Marcel pointed out.

Trust him to remind me of that bitter fact. "If only we had not lost our ancestors' star-drive," she agreed with a mournful sigh. "But we have done so." The ability to send ships between the stars was a lost treasure. "But for that, we could have rebuilt our battle fleets and then extended our holdings into other systems. We could have returned to Arcadia in glory and taken our places as its rightful rulers."

"We have lost much over the centuries."

"And those fools on Cadixia will see us lose more."

"The House Wars?"

"It is as Karul claims." *Damn the man.* "They are draining our culture and resources. We gain honor, but we lose vitality. We must take steps to expand our resource base and our holdings." She gestured to the artwork as if the valuable pieces were even now being threatened by Karul.

"Cadixia is the only habitable world we can reach. The other planets and moons require hostile-environment measures to live there.

Expanding our colonies and holdings among them do have limits. We can mine them for resources, grow food via hydroponics, even live on them, but they remain closed systems."

"I know." She gestured theatrically, playing a role to the other Lord. "Why else would we have so many self-contained colonies? We must have them to survive, but we cannot rely solely upon them to survive forever." The Cadians were spread throughout the system and thus not subject to any easy death through starvation or war or disease...but for how long could they live confined to a single star system? *A few centuries? A few millennia? What then of the future? When the sun dies what will become of the glorious history of our people?*

"What do you recommend then?"

"Waiting for a time longer...then my House will make its move and the Cadian Freeholds will be unified."

"Under *your* rule?"

"Yes." She smiled. "Once the wars are ended, the Cadian People will know peace."

Marcel shook his head. "I do not know that our people would be able to handle peace," he commented dryly. "It is a state foreign to us after all."

"I will make it a priority to divert funding to the scientists of all the Houses. United, working towards a single goal and freely sharing all of their information, surely they can rediscover the secrets of our ancestors' lost star-drive." *United, instead of striving against each other, what might the Cadians accomplish?* "Then we can turn the energies of our people to the stars." The Cadians were skilled soldiers...surely no other world or system could hope to stand against them.

"You do think in grand terms."

"Why else would I bother?" she asked lightly. *Give us new worlds of resources to exploit and time to build up our forces and even the vaunted Republic will be unable to withstand us.* A grand dream true, but one that she or her descendants would one day see fulfilled. *So my family has vowed.*

1 Chapter Seven

"The wars continues to rage beyond this world."

"Yes, Jonathan. War after war after war. There is no end to it."

Jonathan LaLonde turned away from the well-tended flowerbeds. "With a strong leader, the entire Freehold could be like this park."

"A peaceful garden?" Luc Girard shook his head in rueful disbelief. "I find that unlikely," he pointed out. His House colors were mimicked by the flowerbed he stood near. *Did he plan this? An attempt at flattery? Or is this mere coincidence?* LaLonde was crafty...the other Lord must be watched carefully.

"Do you prefer to see the endless wars constantly tearing our culture apart?" Jonathan allowed coldness to seep through his voice. "Every gain we make is lost to the demands of the wars."

"I prefer to see something reasonable. We are a warrior culture. That fact will not change overnight."

"Nonetheless, I wish it to change. I don't want to see the Cadian people—*our* people—doomed to endless warfare. We—they!—deserve better! To be trapped in these cycles of petty warfare until the sun dies? We must move beyond such things and into the greater glory that is our destiny."

"What exactly are you proposing to do?"

There was a long moment of silence while the two Lords paced along the crushed stone pathway. The park was deserted, apart from the two of them.

Jonathan stopped to stare at a fountain. A stylized representation of one of his ancestors stood, with an upraised sword while water jets bubbled from her waist to form a shimmering skirt. "I propose an alliance."

"I've heard that offer before," Luc scoffed. "Many, many times." His eyes drifted to a freighter slowly chugging along the canal. The small flag flying from its bow marked it is as belonging to House LaLonde. "You want to become the Lord of Lords?"

"Someone must guide us."

"So why not you?"

"Who would you prefer?" Jonathan asked candidly. "Would Yvonne Thibeau be more to your liking? Or Jean-Paul Bouchard or Roy Simard?"

"Perhaps I want to see my own House ascendant."

"You don't have the political clout."

"I know." The breeze tugged at his purple-trimmed cloak. He offered a careful smile. "But my House does have some subtle power."

Jonathan looked at him. "You do believe that, don't you?"

"My House and its holdings might not be as large or powerful as your own, or that of Simard or Thibeau, I will grant you that willingly. However, we are not a weakling House either. If another House attacked us, my House might be destroyed," a fact he did not care to admit although it was simple truth, "but the struggle would be long and difficult and the victorious House would be left gutted." Rather than growing stronger, that rival would be left weakened and vulnerable to predation from the other Great Houses in turn.

"We face the piranha principle."

"The *what*?" Luc asked.

"A fish from the past." He had no idea which world had spawned it first, but ancient history files claimed that it now existed on several planets in the greater galaxy. *But is that history truly history, or else merely recorded legend mistaken for truth?* He did not know. "It was a vicious predator which swam in packs. United, they could strip their prey to bone in moments...but if any piranha tried to go off on its own, then its own companions would devour it. Our Houses have the same simultaneous strength and weakness. United we can accomplish much...individually, any House can be destroyed by the strength of the others."

"So we are stuck in this cycle of warfare?"

"Possibly."

"I refuse to believe that we are doomed to these honor wars."

Jonathan shrugged and drew his cloak more tightly around himself as the breeze gusted cold for a moment. "I think that we are...*until* the balance clearly shifts in favor of one House or another." *And then may the ancestors watch over us all.*

* * *

"How long?" Yvonne asked as she sipped juice from a flask. *Wine lacks the usual appeal after being sucked in zero gee*, she thought. *One simply cannot be elegant on long voyages.* But they were necessary if she wished to cultivate the officers and bureaucrats of her House's far-flung holdings.

"Not too long now, my Lady. By the end of the year, or so, we should have sufficient weaponry installed in enough of our ships that we can destroy our foes."

Yvonne smiled. *Bloodthirsty, isn't he?* "It was luck that we gained possession of this asteroid cluster then." *He looks nice in that uniform. The leather molds itself to his arms and chest in a most impressive manner.* She gave herself a mental shake to clear her thoughts. *Business first*, she told herself. *Playtime later.*

"Indeed." Ryan Coleman offered his leader a smile. "Better luck that we have managed to keep control. Starbase Hidden Hope remains viable and almost entirely self-sufficient."

"Yes...how often have the other Houses sought to raid this facility?"

"Only once have any foreign ships breached my security. None of those particular ships reported back to the Tremblays about what they might have seen." His smile shifted to a rather pleased one. "My fighters disabled the *Broadsword* before it could withdraw. My marines secured the ship before it could send a distress signal. We have since refurbished the cruiser and added it to the defences stationed out here."

"Excellent. A most cost effective measure."

"I saw no reason to destroy a two million credit vessel out-of-hand."

"And what of its crew?"

"One hundred and ten of them survived the battle. Seventy of them are still labouring in the mines and ore processing stations."

Yvonne smiled. "I reward officers who show such efficiency."

He offered a quick bow. "My only reward is to serve your House."

"I will keep that in mind, Major."

"Would you like a tour now, my lady?"

"Yes." She nodded. "Show me this vessel that will provide the transport to make my dreams into reality."

* * *

Devin was leaning inside the fuselage of his *Stiletto*. "I got it this time."

"Got what?" Mike asked as he tried to see what his commander was up too.

"I've increased the reactor efficiency."

"That sounds good. By how much, Devin?"

"Point zero one of a per cent."

"Sounds impressive." Mike offered a dry smile. *I heard the technicians bitching about his tinkering. You've burned out two power cores trying to increase reactor efficiency.* "Give it up for a while. You need a break."

"I had a break, back on Cadixia. Went to a bar, remember?"

"Of course I remember. I had to bail you out of that brawl you started."

"I didn't start the brawl." Devin shook his head. "But I sure as hell finished it." He started to laugh, but the sound quickly trailed away. *That arrogant son of a Simard had it coming. I got him good.*

"So take a break now. There's some new vids in the library."

"I'd rather see what the bar has stocked."

"If you want." Mike managed a smile. *At least the galley will limit how much alcohol you can be served,* he thought. *There won't be another repeat of the brawl this time around.*

* * *

"Recover our surviving fighters." Anne-Marie Desroches gave the order in a quiet voice. The battle had been quick and indecisive. Her brigantine, *Desperation*, had encountered a Bouchard cruiser and ordered it to surrender. The captain had refused and the two ships had exchanged several broadsides before the Bouchard vessel broke off and ran.

"Minor hull damage to our port side. Three *Stilettos* lost, two others damaged."

"Their losses?"

"Hull damage, though we're not sure how extensive. They lost six fighters, damage to three others."

"A victory for us then?"

"It seems that way."

Anne-Marie sighed. "These meaningless skirmishes will not advance our House," she commented. "General Thibeau will not smile on us wasting vital military resources for minimal gain."

"We hold the battlefield, Captain. We could have a fighter patrol track the damaged Bouchard fighters and see if they are salvageable."

"Do it." At least it would help replace her own losses. "Comm, prepare a message for broadcast back to Bonavista."

1 Chapter Eight

Yvonne adjusted her purple cloak. "It looks impressive enough." The ship had subtle curves and delicate lines. *Elegance in mechanical form,* she mused. It looked so unlike anything in the current House fleets. The fuselage was a rather elongated, slightly flattened conical form. Three separate clusters of engine nozzles were placed along the aft of the main body, and under the stubby wings. Blisters housed hanger bays and weapon pods. A handful of running lights blinked slowly and other glows marked considerably more portholes than a modern warship would be allowed.

"Its designers were interested in building according to an aesthetic goal, as well as building efficiently," Ryan explained. "Several of the systems are still inoperative."

"It is one of the ancestors' star ships."

"Yes, most definitely."

"Lost out here for centuries..." There was a sense of awe in her voice. "One of a handful of the Exiles to find sanctuary here."

"They didn't find sanctuary, my Lady." Ryan shivered. "The crew starved to death...those who didn't suffocate when the air purifiers went off-line."

She looked at him. "Explain."

"As you already know, we found this ship in the local asteroid cluster." A House-sponsored mining expedition had encountered an anomalous reading during their initial survey. The readings had led them to a derelict star ship. "The boarding crews found the ship in a state of stasis. The reactor was off-line and only a few systems were still functional. The solar collectors were incapable of providing sufficient power to supply everything. The crew appear to have concentrated their energy on life support and propulsion, but it wasn't enough to move the ship very far."

"My father told me little of this."

"I cannot understand why."

"I will speak with him when I return to Bonavista."

Ryan nodded. *If he is still alive.*

"The ship's crew were marooned out here?"

"Yes, my Lady. The *Gauntlet* lost power to its star-drive during its final flight. It ended up drifting out here in the outer system."

"I must read over the logs. I bet they would make for interesting reading."

"Some of them do. Once you get past the archaic language and those accents our ancestors had. We're still decrypting a lot of the operational files. Personal files were easy to access." He offered a shrug. "Security procedures in some areas are quite good. I believe we'll be able to break through the various encryptions in time."

"What House commanded this ship?"

"Christian Entress."

Yvonne frowned. "Entress? I don't recall much about that House."

"From what I have read in the ship's files, it was a minor House on the edge of Arcadia's southern continent. It was initially supportive of Saint-Jamis, before throwing its support behind the Southern Lords as the wars continued." More due to some falling out with the Republic representatives than because Lord Entress truly believed in the traditions and values of the Southern Lords. "The *Gauntlet* was his personal flagship during the Exile."

* * *

Devin sat at the table in the mess hall and picked at his plate. The meal ration was less than appetizing. *I wasn't in the mood for soup,* he thought as he dragged his spoon through the thick broth. *I'm not even sure what flavor it is supposed to be.*

Mike entered the mess hall and received his ration from the server. He came towards Devin's table and plopped into an empty chair. "Alone again, Flight Commander?"

"The heights of command are lonely," Devin replied.

"Only for some. There's plenty of people around here for you to make friends with. You isolate yourself for no reason."

"I'm not much for mingling, Mike."

"I've seen that."

Loud laughter erupted from another table.

"Lieutenant Sommers doesn't have any problems mingling."

Devin glanced towards the laughter. "Jennifer is who she is."

"And you are who you are, Devin." Mike lowered his voice. "You can't change it and you can't keep running away."

"I know that," Devin hissed back. He pushed his bowl of soup away from him. "I've tried and it doesn't work."

"So stop worrying and just live your life."

Devin watched two of the *Reliance's* marines stand up from their table and head towards the doorway. Their dark green uniforms clung to their muscular bodies, rippling as they moved. "Wow," Devin exclaimed. They were both really hunky. *Almost as nice as that Simard officer was.* Mike was still talking, but Devin was no longer listening.

* * *

"Most of the technology on this ship is fairly standard." Ryan Coleman gestured to a bridge display. "We have the same basic communication and weapon systems as our ancestors used."

Yvonne watched technicians working at several stations. Although most of the computer consoles were dark and silent, a handful were humming with power. *I have no idea what they are doing,* she thought. Tests perhaps, or simulations. "The same technology you say?"

"A laser is a laser...the only difference is the efficiency of energy converted to the beam and the amount of waste heat. Conversely, the hardware of the computers is similar to what we currently use, with a few manufacturing differences."

"Nothing we can't replicate?"

"In time. For now, the technicians have been able to jury-rig emergency replacement parts for most of the systems we've been working to restore. Others will require more work, if not replacement."

One technician chose that moment to curse and slap the side of her console with her fist. "You stupid jumble of rusting diodes!" she snapped.

Yvonne looked across the bridge, but the tech was already typing new commands into the keyboard. "It seems that some things never change."

"No, they don't," Ryan admitted sheepishly.

"Our ancestors built good ships if we are able to understand their workings so many centuries later."

"Yes, we can understand them, but don't forget, we never lost the ability to build space craft. The basic techniques are the same for them and for us. What differs is that we have lost some of the refinements since the Exile." He paused a moment. "Thruster efficiency for example—they had better acceleration/deceleration curves than we can manage. Weapon range and power output—these cannons can deliver twice the damage with half the power input."

"Yes, yes. I've seen your reports. I read them on my flight out here." Yvonne nodded. "The ship is very similar to our current designs, with a few slight advances we have yet to rediscover." Those discoveries would come though. *Most of them don't matter yet.* "There is one piece of technology we cannot duplicate. One piece of knowledge that our ancestors lost. The star-drive is what I want."

"The star-drive is useless."

"What?"

Ryan offered her a frown. "Many of the computer records have been corrupted, as you know."

"Some after-effect of the Exile, or so Doctor Trujulo originally believed."

"Yes. Doctor?" Ryan raised his voice and gestured to a white-haired woman standing near one computer console. "Would you care to join us?"

"Of course, Commander. My Lady." The scientist stepped forward. "The *Gauntlet* suffered severe electronic damage," she said in her prim voice. "According to what records we have managed to recover, the convoy passed through a region of space wracked by electromagnetic storms. Radiation and extreme gravitational surges have caused extensive damage. The captain of the *Gauntlet* believed the rest of the convoy suffered similar damage. With his ship's engines damaged he could not maneuver, and with the communication system down, he had no idea the convoy had reached Cadixia safely."

"Can you recover more of the logs?"

"We are trying, my Lady, but after ten years I think that we have learned what secrets we can."

"Many of which we never lost, or else were able to regain. Artificial gravity, the basic inter-planetary drive system, the various sensor systems, etc."

"Yes, quite."

"I *want* a working star-drive."

Coleman and Trujulo looked at each other. "You can't have one."

Yvonne's voice went cold. "I am not accustomed to being denied anything, Doctor."

"I will not promise you something I cannot deliver."

"Why not? You have this ship. You have its star-drive. You have the computer logs."

Doctor Trujillo shook her head. "The *Gauntlet's* star-drive is half-melted wreckage, my Lady. After a decade of work, my staff can't decide what half the technology is, let alone how to repair or replicate it. I can show you the engine room, but you wouldn't understand what you looked at."

"I don't understand how my own *Broadswords* operate," Yvonne admitted, "beyond the basics we learn in our schooling." She could command a ship, but would readily admit that she lacked the technical skills to build or even begin to repair one. "I can't fly a fighter or reprogram a computer. That is why I have staff such as yourself."

"We were trained to work on equipment produced by the various Freeholds. I can obtain technicians capable of repairing House warships and fighters, civilian ships, etc. Our society has the knowledge—the training, the manuals, the experience." Trujillo paused, then shook her head sadly. "But this ship is beyond our knowledge. Without access to the technical records of its construction, we are lost."

"You will have all the funding you need to repair the ship."

"Funding is not an issue. We simply do not possess the knowledge to even begin repairing this ship. We can guess at some of the systems and technologies, as they are similar to what we currently operate, but others remain a mystery to us."

"So this starship is useless then?"

"Hardly," Ryan protested. "Even with its age, the *Gauntlet* is very powerful. We can use the ship to further your plans for the ascension of our House. It will take time, but the future will belong to our House."

"Hidden Hope?"

"Precisely."

1 Chapter Nine

Danielle Nystul handed some coins to a vendor and then sipped from the steaming tea cup. "This is the way to spend a day," she mused.

"At a street fair?" her companion asked.

"Why not, Marc?" The sky was bright and the sun was warm. "It has been a cool spring...the warm weather is finally here."

The nice weather had brought the citizens out in droves. Children and families were mingling in the wide boulevard. Vendors were selling assorted refreshments from carts and tumblers entertained on the street corners. It was a scene of contentment.

"Seems too peaceful for a people constantly at war."

"We're not at war," Danielle replied. "Cadixia is neutral territory. Fighting only happens off world. Out in space or on the colonies. Where it belongs." Her crisp cream-colored uniform did not seem out of place in the open-air café though. Soldiers patrolled many of the streets in the capitol, more from tradition than from a genuine need to maintain the peace.

Marc took a long drink from his own coffee. "The war is coming, you know."

"You've been listening to the general staff again."

"Lady Thibeau is pressing for stronger measures against the other Houses. With the impending death of her father, the entire balance of power between the Houses could shift." The death of the head of a Noble House always led to political flux.

"We're just soldiers. It's not our place to make policy."

"Only to enforce it?"

Marc nodded. "That is why you're wearing the uniform, isn't it?"

She allowed her eyes to gaze at the cityscape. Residential buildings and towers flanked the wide boulevard. "I don't want to see the Freehold in flames," she said.

"Nor do I." Marc looked towards the city's center, where the towers of the House of Lords rose high above every other building. "But we can only enforce the policy determined by our Lords."

* * *

"We'll be sending more ships into the outer system."

Jacques Simard nodded. "To bolster our garrisons or establish new ones?" House assets in the outer regions were limited.

Dennis Simard shook his head. "To do more exploration," he clarified. As head of the House, he was responsible for overall direction and utilization of their assets. "We need an advantage over the others."

"There can't be much else to find. Surely we've explored the system enough by now. We've been here for centuries. Our ships *must* have roamed through every cubic of space by now."

"Jacques, you really must pay more attention to the briefings and less to gossip and carousing."

Jacques flinched. The face of a certain officer flashed before his eyes at the mention of *carousing*. A certain officer of a rival House....

"If you put as much effort into reading technical briefings as you spend maintaining your love life, you would be head of the Admiralty by now."

Jacques shivered. "What a horrible thing to say, Mother. I don't want to be head of the Admiralty."

His parents exchanged glances. "You have a duty to the House. You are bound by the demands of honor to obey."

"I know. I serve in the front lines as much as possible. The *Glorious* has fought nearly twenty-four battles in the last two years."

"Your battle record speaks for itself," Monica Simard said. She had an expression of mingled pride and fear on her face. Her dark hair was bound in an intricate braid which hung over her left shoulder.

Dennis Simard had only pride on his age-lined face. "That is one reason you are being placed in command of the task force. This is not simply because you are Simard."

"I don't think that I have been given a command or mission simply based on my bloodline," Jacques replied. *I've always trained harder than anyone else just to prove that I deserve any promotion I received. I am not riding on my family's name.*

"No one questions your ability," Roy Simard announced from his chair halfway down the narrow conference table. "But you must accept that you are destined for more than merely commanding a warship."

"I know that." *But I'm not going to stop fighting that final promotion for as long as I can.* He let his brown eyes scan the other officers seated along both sides of the table. *They all look content with their places in the grand scheme. Am I the only one who wants more?*

"Then if we can continue the briefing?" Dennis called the meeting back to order. As the House officers and nobles turned their attention to him, he took a breath and gestured to the wall-mounted view screen. "The outer system is vast and barren. Patrols tend to be isolated and often fall prey to ambushes by rival Houses...."

* * *

"Welcome home, my Lady."

"Thank you, General Thibeau." Yvonne nodded politely to the old man. "I appreciate you meeting me here, Uncle."

"You are the leader of our House. I serve as best I can." He fell into step beside her as they walked across the platform from the shuttle. "I trust you had a safe journey?"

"Yes, Uncle. Not even a single enemy raid to alleviate the boredom."

"I'm certain you will soon find new ways to excite yourself."

"My father's health is growing worse?"

"Yes."

The hint of a smile played around Yvonne's mouth. "Have those silly rumors of poisoning gone away yet?"

"A few whispers are still making the rounds of the court," Lucien admitted. "Suppression of the rumor mongers continues."

"Excellent. I want those vicious lies laid to rest. I will not have my father's final days disturbed."

"Yes, my Lady."

"Major Coleman was most informative."

"His reports have always been so."

"When the *Jeweled Gauntlet* is ready for combat, place him in command."

"As you wish."

"He has served our House efficiently. I wish him rewarded."

Lucien nodded. "I will arrange for the appropriate mission orders."

"Speaking of the *Gauntlet*, how long before the bulk of our fleet can be upgraded with the new weapon designs?"

"Work is already proceeding at the Citroen Shipyards. A fleet-wide upgrade will take time and money. The risk of discovery is great." The other Houses would eventually notice the enhanced firepower Thibeau warships possessed. "Perhaps we should reconsider spreading out the weapons. If we concentrate the new weapons on our home world garrison, as well as the reserves, it will limit the risk of discovery."

"My father wanted the weapons widely deployed."

"Your father is no longer making decisions for our House," Lucien reminded her. "The fate of House Thibeau is in your hands...and you are not as wise in the ways of the universe as I."

"I know, Uncle." Yvonne smiled at him. "Very well. I shall concede to your superior knowledge of tactics. Limit the spread of the new technology to whatever units you deem safe."

"I will focus on the Reserve for now." Lucien knew that was the best policy for now. "None of the other Houses know the full strength of our military. I promise you that." *None of my agents have ever reported any rumors to me about other Houses knowing just how many ships we can field.* "Your father has been building up the Reserve for some time. He has been keeping the Reserve deployed to our outer holdings and on long patrols, away from the other Houses. When we deploy our full military strength, no other House will be able to match us."

"We will out-gun all others?"

"I believe we will be able to match the combined fleets of at least three other Houses in direct combat. With the Reserve units equipped with superior automation and weaponry, we will be able to field a larger number of ships without a correspondingly high number of crewers. Whether that will make up for combat experience, I do not know." *Training only goes so far...we can hardly send out thousands of new crewers for the other Houses to see. Without actual combat experience, training only prepares a soldier so much.*

"Accelerate the refurbishment of the Reserve. I see little reason to delay our operations."

"Yes, my Lady."

She heard his tone. "You disapprove?"

"I urge caution. We have been preparing for decades, ever since finding the *Gauntlet*. Our House has been planning and plotting its ascension for centuries before that. We are entering a critical time...I do not wish to see this House stumble and all that planning and waiting be wasted."

"I agree...but I also refuse to cower cautiously when there is no need. We have waited centuries...I will not wait millennia."

"Hidden Hope is a vital resource for our House. I will squander it."

"Nor will I, Uncle. Nor will I."

1 Chapter Ten

Devin cursed loudly as one of his wingmen died in a bright and quickly extinguished fireball. "We're out-numbered already!" he snarled. "Emerald flight, respond!" The comm-system crackled with static. "There'd better be someone out there who can hear me. I'd hate to think I was the only one left." He flipped his fighter end-over-end and fired his lasers at a pursuing *Stiletto*. "Come on guys, respond!"

"*...erald Flight...break...out-number...treat...*"

"Say again. Repeat, say that again?" Devin adjusted his comm, but could only raise static. "Control? Are you there, *Reliance*?"

A laser burned through his starboard wing.

Fighting thrown into a sharp spin, Devin cursed as alarms sounded. *Fuel line breach,* he noted from the flashing diagnostic displays. *Engine power loss. Laser cannon off-line.* "Not good..." he mumbled. He triggered one of his last remaining missiles, watched it acquire a target and streak away, then he turned his attention to trying to fly his damaged fighter and keeping an eye on the battlefield.

His tactical display was littered with dozens of starfighters zipping about in all directions, exchanging laser bolts and missiles. A dozen fighters were drifting with zero power emissions. Three of the freighters the LaLonde patrol had attempted to capture were now drifting hulks, either crippled by the battle or else boarded by marines. One freighter was accelerating away from the battle at maximum thrust. *On a vector for Miser,* Devin noted with a smile. *We got one.* Two more freighters were still moving on their original course, flanked by two *Broadswords* and several fighter squadrons.

He didn't see the *Reliance's* beacon on his screen and that worried him. "Where is everyone?" He was moving towards one of the drifting freighters. "Maybe I can dock with it." He was running low on oxygen. *Must have taken a hit earlier in the battle.*

Two *Stilettos* dove past him without firing. They were marked with the colors of House Simard, adding to Devin's confusion. "Where did the Simards come from?" he wondered. Last report he had received from the *Reliance* was that the patrol was closing on a Bouchard patrol and freighter convoy. *Did the* Reliance *get it wrong?* he wondered. *Or has Simard joined forces with Bouchard?* Not that any alliance between the Houses would last for long of course. *They never do.*

The comm crackled once again, but this time a voice came through without static. "*This is HSS* Glorious *to all remaining LaLonde pilots. Your* Sheathe *has withdrawn. Surrender immediately and I promise that you will be well treated. Resist and you die.*"

Devin sighed. "Not much choice left to me then." The heads-up display was empty of friendly transponder beacons. *Either I'm the last one left, or the others are out of range.* He frowned at the thought and tried to think of the many reasons for the lack of the transponders. *Battle damage. Out of my fighter's scanner range. Powerless and drifting.* He checked his own *Stiletto's* systems, but warning lights were still flashing. *Missiles gone. Fuel levels low. Oxygen reserves at critical.* "This Emerald Leader. I surrender."

* * *

"Takes us forward."

"As you command, my Lady." Personally, Ryan would have preferred to have been commanding the flagship without his Lady being present on the observation deck watching his every move and offering her suggestions. *She does not have military training. She is a distraction I can ill afford.* But she was his ruler and he could not contradict her.

"This is our first test and we must make it a good one."

"As you command, my Lady."

She stared through a viewport at a passing asteroid. "If the meeting with Lord Tessier does not come to prove as fruitful as I hope, then this test will be of paramount importance."

"Captain, we have detected freighters bearing to port."

"Order them to heave too."

"No response."

Yvonne turned. "Lock port lasers on target...disable their engines."

"Do it," Ryan ordered.

"Targets locked."

"Fire at will."

"Direct hits on both targets! Threat eliminated."

Yvonne smiled. "Excellent shooting," she called out. *Direct hits at twice normal weapons' range...this ship truly is a marvel of engineering.* The other secrets it contained would be deciphered in time and her House would dominate the Freehold and beyond.

* * *

The bustle of a court meeting was normally busy. The interaction of courtiers and officers made for a costumed dance.

Jonathan LaLonde chuckled at the thought of his court as some absurd theatrical production. Still, as he stood on the balcony overlooking the sunken floor where technicians worked at computer terminals and small clumps of men and woman talked quietly, the thought persisted.

"Something amuses you, my Lord?"

Jonathan turned his head. "Just a momentary thought, Damian. Nothing of importance." *My own clothing would not seem out of place amid such a performance,* he noted with a mental chuckle.

Damian nodded once and returned to studying the stack of hardcopy documents in his hands. "We might have to deal with an incursion near the refinery at Arabay."

"Is it being threatened?"

"The gas giant is a natural refueling point. Several of the other Houses maintain their own stations there. Security at our own is growing eclipsed by the combined strength of the others."

"Dispatch another patrol to bolster our garrison then." He could not afford to lose that refinery. *A secure source of fuel is vital for my warships and commercial fleet to be able to move freely throughout the Freehold. Without fuel, my ships would be confined to orbit around their bases.*

"As soon as I can figure out where to route them from." Deployments of the House Military were never quick choices. *Weaken one spot and the other Houses will pounce in an instant to seize it for themselves.*

A woman in a courier's uniform approached. "My Lord?"

Jonathan turned his head. "Yes, Lieutenant?" he asked in a casual tone of voice.

"We have just received word from Bonavista. Lord Thibeau is dead."

The room went silent.

"He was a worthy foe. He never yielded to a rival, not for an instant." Jonathan LaLonde lowered his head for a moment of quiet prayer. "Once, we might have stood as allies against the other Houses."

"What happened to prevent such an alliance?" Damian asked as the courier stepped off the balcony to return to her own duties.

"He wanted to rule, I wanted to rule. The usual political complications." Jonathan raised his glass towards the ceiling in a final toast. "I wonder if his daughter will live up to his reputation."

"So far she has done an admirable job of holding their Freehold together during his long illness."

"True." *But how does that bode for the future? With her father still alive, no one would question her. With him dead, how strong is her hold over the rest of her House? Is there a cousin or an aunt to contest the right of succession?* If there was, an intra-House civil war would leave their holdings vulnerable. *I must keep an eye on that House,* he thought to himself.

The bustle of the room returned to normal.

"We have been unable to regain contact with the *Reliance*. I fear the ship is lost."

"I see. Contact the *Green Knight* and have the entire patrol sweep their area of space for the *Reliance*. Order the *Knight* to withdraw rather than be destroyed should it encounter significant enemy strength."

"Yes, Lord."

"We've lost enough from that engagement that I will not waste more resources on a fool's errand."

"Yes, Lord. We still have two *Broadswords* operating out there. The battle was not a complete failure though. We inflicted significant damage onto the Bouchard convoy and we did manage to take possession of two heavily laden freighters. One other freighter was scuttled beyond recovery, or else captured by House Simard. We're not sure which. House Bouchard only recovered two of its five freighters. The minerals gained more than pay for the fighters and ships lost in the battle."

"Perhaps." Jonathan shook his head. "I suppose it was a victory then."

"By this accounting, my Lord, it was."

"By other accounts, it cost us in resources and lives."

"Our pilots know the risks. They know what it means when their ships go into battle. No patrol can ever be garuanteed risk free."

"I will not squander the lives of my pilots. Never forget that, Damian."

"Of course not, my Lord." He sounded surprised by the insinuation.

Jonathan allowed a servant to refill his glass. "What other matters demand my urgent attention?" he asked.

l Chapter Eleven

"Devin Shaw. I thought I recognized your picture."

Sprawled on a small cot, Devin finally looked up. "You!" he gasped. He had heard the door open, but chosen to ignore it. *I thought it would either be more bland prison food or an interrogator. This is a nice surprise.*

"It's been a long time since *Baxter's.*" Jacques smirked as he stared down at the man laying before him. "I never expected to see you again, let alone have you become a guest in my brig." *Those prison coveralls do not do him justice,* he thought.

"I didn't know this was your ship."

"Otherwise you would have tried to blow it up?"

"It wouldn't be anything personal."

"Of course not. Just business as usual?" Jacques glanced through the open door, but the guard in the corridor was just standing there silently. "I trust the accommodations are comfortable?"

"Yeah. I won't be staying here long though."

"No, you won't."

Devin's expression paled at the swift reply. He stared back at the Simard captain. *That uniform looks tailor-made for him.* He had the skin coloring to make the blue-with-yellow-trim uniform perfect. *A vid-director would kill for an actor who looked that good in uniform. The House recruiting department would pay a fortune for him on their posters. Hell, if I saw him in the window of a recruitment post, I'd go in.* Devin gave himself a quick mental shake. "What's it going to be, Jacques?" he asked, making his voice cold and harsh. "Sentenced to a mining asteroid? Or a quick execution?"

Jacques looked startled by the tone. "I'll probably ransom you back to House LaLonde," he replied with a scornful laugh. "We might get a new *Stiletto* or two for you."

Devin laughed bitterly. "I think you value me more highly than my House does."

Jacques turned and walked back out of the cell. The door hissed closed.

* * *

"Lord Tessier, I suggest that you look at the current political landscape." Yvonne Thibeau gestured at the lush gardens around them. "It is changing as rapidly as my gardens." Her staff had been laboring for weeks to convert part of the park into a monument to her late father. The statue was still being carved, but the pedestal was ready and the grove of trees would look as if it had been standing ready for decades.

"I have seen it, Yvonne."

She turned towards him, knowing that her lilac dress stood out against the painted ferns. Even for this walk in the garden, her hair was coiffed into an intricate coiled braid and she wore a minimum of jewelry. "Then you must see that it is just as the others have claimed in the Conclaves. Continuing these internecine wars is only serving to weaken our Houses. We must have unity if we are too truly hope to reclaim the technology of our ancestors."

"Perhaps." Max Tessier adjusted the fall of his fur-line gray cloak. "But why should the new First Lord of Lords be yourself?" His own green tunic and pants caused him to blend into the vegetation.

Yvonne paused in mid-step. "Why?" she asked, turning towards her fellow Lord.

"What qualifies you to take possession of the Freehold?" He calmly plucked one of the brilliant blue blooms from a laden rose bush and inhaled the delicate scent.

"House Thibeau was a power on Arcadia. My family ruled one of the largest city-states there, before Saint-Jamis sought off-world aid to seize total control."

"Ah, but my own family controlled a city-state. All of our Noble Houses did."

Yvonne's eyes narrowed. "House Thibeau was the largest and most powerful of them." *Saint-Jamis notwithstanding.*

"That was a thousand years ago. Things change."

"And some things remain constant."

"Possibly."

"I have the support of several Houses already, Max. It is only a matter of time before the rest of the others join me. Or give way to the inevitable." She paused a moment, licking her full lips. "I can be most *generous* to friends of my House."

"I'm certain you can be. In that respect you have proven to be a worthy heir to your father. I remain unconvinced of your suitability however."

Yvonne drew herself to her full height. "Is that your final word?" she demanded in a cold voice.

"For now it is."

"Perhaps you should return to Maraselle then." With an effort, she made her tone more calm once again. "We can discuss this matter later."

Max offered her a polite bow. "We can discuss it as often as you like, Yvonne, but my mind will not be changed by words alone. Actions do speak louder than words you know."

Her blue eyes narrowed. "Good day then, Lord Tessier."

* * *

Phil Sullivan stared at the words glowing on the display. "Dead?" He could scarcely believe the words on the screen. "Our Lord is dead?"

"The message has been confirmed." Neil Latimer nodded. "The illness was incurable."

"I will make an announcement to our staff later."

"Of course, Colonel."

"Is there anything else I need to be aware of?"

"Just the routine supply run. The message was deemed important enough to carry here in person."

"My thanks for that." Starbase Hidden Hope was a hidden facility, and its main defense was its secrecy.

"I have no further word from Lady Yvonne."

"We are continuing to operate as per her last instructions." *Decipher the secrets of the ancestor's starship and apply them to the House Navy. House Thibeau must become strong.* "Any word of rebellion?" *Always a risk when a ruler dies...the other Houses are quick to prey on any sign of weakness.*

"Nothing that I heard when I left Cadixia. Our holdings remain securely committed to House Thibeau."

"Thanks for that. A civil war would destroy us."

"I think everyone knows that. None of the petty nobles are foolish enough to risk the destruction of our House."

"Yvonne will have her work cut out for her. The other Lords are playing at politics and she's not completely up to speed. Her father was a hard man."

"A harsh man."

"But he knew how to keep his House in order. I don't know if Yvonne has his patience."

"Will you have any dispatches for me to carry back to Bonavsita?" Neil asked.

"Probably," Phil replied. "Go and see to your crew's needs, Captain, while I have your cargo unloaded."

"Thank you, Colonel."

1 Chapter Twelve

"The *Glorious* should reach Cartier Station in another day or so."

Devin nodded. "And that is where you'll dump me?"

"That is where you will be turned over to the appropriate authorities. A short stay and you should be repatriated to your own House."

Devin chewed at his lip for a moment. "I don't really want to leave."

"You can hardly stay here forever. Space in the brig is quite limited and legitimate prisoners will need to use it eventually." Jacques chuckled. "Of course, you are still my prisoner as well."

"I know."

Jacques stood up and slowly turned around. "I should get back to the bridge." He gave his uniform tunic a tug to straighten it. "We'll be arriving at the freighter in a few minutes."

"I guess I should go back to what I was doing before you invited me to play chess." Devin gestured to the abandoned board. "You are a very skilled player."

"Chess is symbolic warfare. As a ship captain, I should have a good head for tactics and strategy."

Devin grinned. "Yep."

The door hissed open. "Return him to his quarters, Sergeant Adler," Jacques ordered briskly.

The marine nodded. "Yes, Captain."

Devin stepped into the corridor and began to walk towards the lift. "Back to the boredom of my cell."

"At least you get to leave it periodically. Not many prisoners get guided tours of the captain's quarters."

"I know." They walked further along the corridor. "How's the wrist today, Tony?"

"It's better," the marine replied. "A little sore still, but improving."

Devin had gotten to know his usual marine escort quite well over the last few weeks. *I feel more comfortable here than I ever did on the* Reliance. *A most unusual feeling.*

An alarm sounded.

Tony tensed as a voice from the intercom ordered the crew to battle stations. "We should hurry."

Devin offered a shy grin. "If you need to get to your battle station, I can find my own way back to my cell."

Tony laughed. "No doubt, but I should escort you there myself. Orders, you know."

"I know." Devin chuckled. "Worth a try, I suppose."

"A good one too, but we really should—whoa!" He cried out as the deck lurched under the feet. Both men were thrown against the bulkhead.

Devin shook his head. "Something hit us." He half stood up. "You okay, Tony?" The marine was sprawled on the deck and didn't answer and Devin hastily crawled to his side. "You okay?" *At least he's still breathing.* "Tony, say something?" Devin reached for the man's comm-link. "Marine down. Medical to detention."

The *Glorious* lurched again.

"What's going on?"

Jacques cursed loudly as the fighters made another pass. "We got suckered in," he snarled. The freighter was a cunning trap. *At least I made it to the bridge before the shooting started.* He could go down with his ship if it came to that. "Status report?"

"Hull breach in two forward sections. Casualties are being reported."

"Target those fighters. All point defense batteries are cleared for independent control." *Where is the enemy?* "Target that freighter!"

"Repair crews are responding."

"Target on tracking…it's moving away."

Running so soon? "They're no match for a real warship. Just a Thibeau trick." Send a distress signal reporting fighter attack and when a warship responds, the freighter unleashes a missile barrage from hidden launch ports. *Clever too—a few well-placed hits from the surprise attack and a real warship would be half-crippled before the battle begins.* "They won't catch any other ships like this." He would see to that. "Comm, transmit a report to Cartier Station. Notify them of this treachery."

"Yes, Captain."

"Fresh missiles incoming."

"Point defense?"

"Intercepting now."

"Target that damned freighter!" His eyes locked onto the icon moving across the display screen. "*Wooden Duck*, eh? *Sitting Duck* is more accurate. Fire!" His *Sheath's* heavy lasers stabbed out at the freighter. "Where's my fighter support?" he demanded.

"Not sure, Captain."

"Find out and quickly!"

Devin finished fastening his helmet as the door closed behind him. *I must be crazy,* he thought. *But I'd rather die in a fighter than trapped helpless on this ship.* The borrowed—all right, *stolen*—flight suit was loose on him, but it would have to do. *I didn't want to linger in the flight lounge in case any of the real Simard pilots showed up.*

The hanger deck was the same as on any LaLonde ship. A dozen *Stilettos* were sitting on the deck, waiting for their pilots to arrive.

"Move it!" a flight technician shouted as Devin entered the bay. "We need every ship we can launch." He stepped away from a fighter. "It's primed and ready for launch."

"Got it!" Devin called back. He climbed into the already prepped fighter and sealed the cockpit. *Good thing the* Stiletto *is a standardized design*, he thought to himself. The cockpit had the same exact control panels as his own destroyed craft. "This will be a snap." He began the preflight checklist.

"No time for that!" Flight Ops informed him. "Launch!"

Devin felt the magnetic catapult kick his fighter into space. He powered up the engines and sent the *Stiletto* into a sharp roll. "Yep, just like my old one." The power plant was a bit more efficient than that in his former fighter. *Better technician or a new advance in the technology?* The Houses maintained their own technical tricks and secrets for as long as was possible, though spies were everywhere and post-battlefield salvage was common.

"Thibeau fighters have rallied. The squadron is coming in from port."

Jacques cursed. "Our weakest side." The port side had already taken multiple hits missile from the ambush and many of the point defense batteries were disabled. "Evasive maneuvers." Previous attack runs had cost the Thibeau six *Stilettos* destroyed or disabled, but the survivors were persistent.

"Rapier Flight is moving to intercept."

Jacques winced. *If things were less desperate, I would order my pilots to stay close to the* Glorious. Six fighters against fifteen was a recipe for disaster. "Flag to all pilots...good luck." It was all he could offer.

"*Luck?*" a voice cracked over the comm. "*Luck has nothing to do with it. Let me show you how a real pilot flies.*"

Jacques frowned. *That's no way for a pilot to talk to me.*

"That wasn't Rapier-Three."

"Identify that man!" Jacques demanded.

"Yes, Captain."

"Rapier-Three is moving to engage."

"Get me a visual!"

Devin triggered his launcher and sent two *Adder*-class missiles streaking towards the Thibeau ships. "At least I'm not trying to fly through a LaLonde group." They would never accept him in a stolen fighter and probably shoot him down before he could make them believe he really was a member of their House. *Out here, everyone's my enemy.* He laughed bitterly.

A laser burned past his wing.

The comm-system crackled. "*Rapier-Three, identify yourself.*"

Devin tapped the comm. "This is Rapier-Three. Who do you think I am?" *I have no idea who the hell I'm supposed to be. The tech never told me who he thought I was.*

"*You aren't Rapier-Three.*"

"I'm a little busy right now. Can we talk later?" He flipped the fighter end-over-end and burned in pursuit of a Thibeau *Stiletto*. "Rapier-Three out."

Jacques frowned as Rapier-Three broke the transmission. "It can't be," he muttered. *How did he get to the flight deck so quickly?* Yet, it could only be Devin. Medical had found his escort unconscious and so far no sign of the prisoner had been found. *No time to order a full ship-wide search for one man either,* he thought. *Not with this battle raging.* He doubted Devin would try to sabotage the *Glorious*, not if doing so risked getting himself killed in a doomed ship. "It must be him in that fighter."

"Who, Captain?"

"Devin Shaw."

"The prisoner?" Michelle Reeve frowned. "But how?"

"He's the only person I can think of who might be out there."

The *Katana's* first officer shook her head. "Is this an escape attempt?"

"I doubt it." Jacques couldn't see it. "He already knows that we plan to ransom him back to his own House. Why risk his life trying to flee from us in a stolen fighter? We're still in open space." *Devin would know that a fighter lacks the fuel and life support range to reach any planet or colony. Unless he stumbles across another ship or a completely unknown space station he has no hope of getting away from us.*

"Panic?"

"He willingly stole a fighter and then charged at the enemy. Right now, he's dog fighting a numerically superior force. I don't think he's panicking." *He's good too.* "If he was trying to escape, why choose a short-range fighter? Better to have tried stealing one of the shuttles." *Still a doomed effort...a shuttle would not get far.*

The tactical officer raised his voice. "*Wooden Duck* has been disabled." It was drifting. A visual showed atmosphere leaking from numerous breaches and several large holes marred the aft section. "The crew are ejecting."

"Good shooting."

"The dogfight is continuing."

"Casualties?"

"We've lost four pilots. Thibeau has lost seven to the fighters, three more to point defense."

"Order the Thibeau pilots to surrender. Without their freighter as a base, those fighters don't have enough life support or fuel to reach any planet or station." A drawback of a short-range design, but not one which could be easily remedied. "They will surrender or die."

"Transmitting now."

"This is HSS Glorious *to all Thibeau fighters. Your freighter is disabled and its crew are ejecting in lifepods. The battle is lost. Surrender and*

disarm your weapon systems. We will recover you and ransom you back to your House. Continue to resist and you will be shot down."

Devin nodded at the words. "They have no choice." The battle had been vicious, but he was unharmed. *So is my fighter. At least I get to return it in pristine condition.* That might make the Simard technicians happy. *I wonder what mood the* Glorious's *captain will be in?* Jacques was rather cute when he was mad.

The Thibeau fighters were signaling their surrenders now and moving towards the *Glorious* for recovery.

A shuttle launched from the *Katana*, heading towards the now-disabled freighter to recover the drifting lifepods.

"*Rapier-Three, you are cleared for landing.*"

"Acknowledged, *Glorious.*" Devin brought his borrowed *Stiletto* in for a landing. Like all fighter-to-ship landings, he just brought the fighter towards the hanger bay and matched velocity and speed with the *Sheath*; its tractor beam pulled him inside and into the appropriate berth. *Easy.* He felt tired. *Too long out of a cockpit. I'm getting soft.*

Technicians hurried to assist him in climbing out of the cockpit.

1 Chapter Thirteen

"Open fire."

Such a simple command, Yvonne Thibeau thought as she stood near the main display screen onboard the *Jeweled Gauntlet*. Too simple perhaps, given that it issued in the dawn of a new era for the Cadian Freeholds. *But is the best command I can give at the moment.*

One of the floor-to-ceiling displays showed an overview of local space, with a dozen Thibeau warships in orbit above the planetoid. A secondary display tracked the last of the crippled defenders as a Tessier frigate tumbled out of orbit and sank into the planetoid's gravitational embrace.

The main display showed the surface of Maraselle.

The surface was barren gray rock and dust—a typical asteroid. Craters pockmarked the airless world, though none of them were more recent than ten thousand years. The planet was one of the system's more useless hunks of rock. Few mineral resources worth the effort of mining; no water deposits; no self-sustaining biosphere; no significant reasons for Humanity to establish a home there.

Nonetheless, a series of interconnected domes covered the main city from which House Tessier ruled its holdings, though many of the structures were actually located underground. It was a planet with gravity however, and that made it somewhat valuable.

Yvonne smiled as her ships began firing. Missiles rained down onto the surface of Maraselle. The colony had refused to surrender to her, despite her repeated demands, and now it would pay the ultimate price. *I regret that some must die today...but their sacrifice will convince others not to oppose my will. I have no desire to see the other Freeholds suffer. This star system* must *be unified...under* my *rule.*

"Fresh signals from the planet, my Lady."

She turned. "Yes, Major?"

Ryan Coleman stepped to her side. "The signals are coming on all emergency channels."

"Lord Tessier has seen the error of his way?" Yvonne asked calmly. Her lilac jumpsuit was reminiscent of military fatigues. "He wishes to pledge his service to my House?"

"Not exactly. The first missile strike breached the primary dome. The capitol city is in an uproar." That calm statement masked a bitter truth. *The death toll among the civilians would be high.*

"He should have accepted my offer when it was made back on Cadixia."

"My Lady, you have proven the superiority of your fleet. You destroyed his patrols without apparent effort or losses to your patrols. This barrage of a mostly civilian population will gain you no support in the Conclaves."

"Do not question my decisions, Major. I am in charge of this House." Her voice cracked like a whip. "I do what I must and the far-reaching results of my every decision will not always be obvious to my subordinates."

Ryan Coleman nodded at the rebuke. "Yes, my Lady."

"Tessier knew the risks when he turned down my offer. An example must be made."

"It is a costly one."

"The deaths here will prevent further deaths," Yvonne told him in a calm voice. "Other Houses will see the consequences of opposing me and they will accept my assumption of the First Lordship." *They would have no choice.*

* * *

"You fought well out there."

"I didn't want to die."

"So you climbed into a cheap fighter?"

"Two and ten hundred thousand credits is cheap?"

"I meant," Jacques said calmly, "that you left a warship for a fighter?"

Devin chuckled. "I'd rather die fighting on my own terms. If the ship took a hit, I'd be dead before even knowing I was in danger. In a *Stiletto*, I can try to dodge."

Jacques ran his fingers across Devin's chest. "I was worried about you."

"And I thought you'd be mad. Thinking I was trying to escape." He snuggled closer against Jacques. "This is not the welcome back I expected." He adjusted the sheets covering them. "But I like it."

"It's not what I planned either," Jacques admitted dryly. "I don't usually sleep with my pilots."

"You just sleep with the enemy?"

"I don't think sleep is in our immediate future," Jacques told him with a sudden grin.

* * *

Small pleasure craft chugged under the arcing bridge. The sunlight was warm that morning.

"I haven't ridden in a boat like that for years."

"Perhaps you should arrange one, my Lord."

Lord Jonathan LaLonde chuckled at the suggestion. "I doubt that my security advisors would permit it."

Bianca Tremblay smiled back at him. "Nor would mine." She laughed softly. "They were against this little meeting as well."

"A diplomatic meeting?"

"In carefully chosen neutral ground." Bianca looked around the Park of Ever-Singing Nightingales. "We are quite safe, I'm certain. Our security teams have been through here ahead of us." And a cordon of guards had been stationed around the two nobles. *Far enough away to be out of our sight, but close enough to be handy should we require rescue. Even in a meeting seeking peace, we plot for war.*

"The House of Lords looks nice from this angle."

"It does." The mid-morning sun was catching the stonework and roof tiles and the main tower glittered like a jeweled scepter. "What did you wish to come from this meeting?"

"I merely wished to see you, Bianca. The Conclaves are hardly a fitting for place for idle small talk."

"You do not seem the type to desire *idle small talk*." She paused to read the inscription in front of one tall statue. "Nor does the setting of this Park strike me as a place you would willingly come."

"I can be as desirous of peace as anyone else." Jonathan gestured at the statue. "Constance Schiller sought to bring peace."

"A pity she was assassinated by your House."

"That was never proven," Jonathan snapped. "It's a lie."

"Is it? Your House paid for most of her statue."

"My House has paid for many statues."

"And many warships."

He frowned. "Bianca," he called by her first name, "the Resource Wars have raged between our Houses for centuries...surely you can see how useless they are. How utterly meaningless and destructive to our people."

She made no reply.

"You raised that very point at the Conclave."

"My people *are* tired of war, Lord LaLonde. They are tired of hearing about the deaths of their fellows on distant colonies. Tired of the constant suspicion of outsiders. Tired of pirate raids." Her mouth twitched at that. There were no real pirates, just secret House-sponsored *rogue* ships. "We want an end to these Wars."

"I have been talking with other nobles about that very thing," Jonathan told her. "With your help, an end to the Resource Wars could be closer than *any* of us suspect."

She looked at him, her expression openly studying his face. "Do go on," she prompted as birds sang in the tree branches above her head.

* * *

Cartier Station was slowly rotating as the *Glorious* approached it. The disk-shaped station gleamed in the starlight. A dozen cruisers and brigantines drifted like miniature moons.

"There it is."

"It's a fairly uninspired design."

"It is larger than anything *your* House has built." Jacques chuckled. "Bigger is better."

Devin smiled. "You just keep telling yourself that."

"It's a major trading hub for the part of the system. Several of our mining colonies rely on *Cartier* for shipping their ore in-system. Or for obtaining vital supplies for continued operations among the outer planets." He raised his voice. "Comm, signal *Cartier* for docking instructions."

"Aye, Captain."

"Then alert the station commander that I want to arrange a conference." Arriving at the station was important. "We'll have to arrange for repairs." *And shore leave for the crew. They deserve some time to themselves.*

Devin watched the displays. *Three patrols of warships seems hardly enough defensive garrison for a space station as important as Cartier was rumored to be. Then again, I have no idea what integral firepower it has to protect itself. Probably dozens of weapon batteries covering every angle of attack.* The number of civilian freighters in orbit or docked was also impressive. *I had no idea Simard commanded* that *many ships.* Surely their merchant marine could not be so big!

Jacques was still issuing orders to his crew.

Devin paused a moment as he examined the displays. *Those aren't all Simard ships!* he thought. The colorings and markings were quite plain. *So House Tessier trades out here too.* And wasn't that a *LaLonde* ship?

1 Chapter Fourteen

Once the *Glorious* was docked in a shipway, Jacques left the bridge. "Coming, Devin?"

"Coming?"

"Aboard the station. Or are you not yet sick of being onboard the ship?"

Devin hurried after his friend. "I thought I was still your prisoner."

"*Cartier* is a possession of House Simard. Onboard the *Glorious* or *Cartier*, where are you going to escape too?" he paused. "I can assure you that the hanger bays on *Cartier* will be more closely guarded than those on my ship were during the battle."

"I'll come along then."

"Good, I was hoping you'd see it my way."

"Good to see you again, Jacques." The woman was wearing a tight leather jumpsuit, which empathized the slender curves of her body. Her brown hair had been woven into an intricate braid which was then coiled atop her head. Her eyes flicked briefly over at Devin as he followed Jacques through the airlock.

"Melissa, it has been too long." Jacques offered her a polite bow.

She nodded to him. "Charming as ever I see." Her smile was warm and welcoming, genuine not merely a polite greeting. "And who is your handsome friend?"

"Devin Shaw, Flight Commander of the House LaLonde Military."

Melissa shot a startled look towards Jacques, then gave Devin a longer study. "He's cute, though hardly the type I would have expected to see with you." She was obviously studying the LaLonde officer. "And you have brought him because?"

"He was a prisoner of war."

"*Was?*"

"Now he is my guest."

"As you wish. You and your crew and your guests are welcome on my station." Her voice chilled. "Still, I would suggest that keep your guest away from the restricted sections of *Cartier* or he will be shot on sight by security."

"Trust me, I'll keep clear." Devin gave her a half-hearted smile.

"Good." Melissa smiled back, though this time the expression lacked her earlier warmth. "This way then." She led them along the corridor and into a small office. "We can talk here."

"Thank you for the privacy." Jacques looked around, but the office only contained a few chairs and a small desk. *Merely a customs booth really.*

"Somethings are best not discussed in public corridors. Now, I see that the *Glorious* took a little beating."

Jacques nodded as he took one of the chairs for himself. "We tangled with a LaLonde patrol first, then got jumped by a Thibeau ambush."

"I read your report on that before you docked. Nasty little trick they played on you. I wonder how many other ships they've seized with their *Wooden Duck*?"

"No idea."

"The repairs are easy enough to make. A week or so should see the *Glorious* back to its usual pristine condition. My technical staff is at your disposal, of course. You needed replacement fighters?"

"If you have any to spare."

"I think I can muster a half flight for you. The rest will have to await your return to a better stocked military base."

"I thought you kept extras of everything out here."

"I try too, but lately my supply shipments have been disrupted. Thibeau and Graham are striking at every convoy in this sector. My escorts are being strained trying to keep up with all the traffic we tend to attract."

"Maybe I should send the *Glorious* on a little cruise."

"I would appreciate that."

"Is *Cartier* in danger?" Devin asked.

"No," Melissa replied instantly. "Certainly not."

Jacques shook his head. "The others are trying a fairly standard ploy of starving us slowly by cutting off our supply lines." Basic tactics for any style of warfare. "*Cartier* has vast stockpiles of supplies, to say nothing to sufficient armaments to fend off a major multi-patrol attack."

"No other House has ever taken control of this station," Melissa informed them in a cold tone. "I have defended *Cartier* from more than two dozen raids in the last twenty years. Only once did a rival House penetrate the defenses to land troops...and none of them advanced past the first level of bulkheads. None of the invaders withdrew alive."

"Good work then."

"I almost welcome a challenge. If Thibeau or Graham attempts to capture this station, none of their ships will survive the attempt."

"Better to fight here, then continue to raid our shipping. Not that they will see it that way."

"Thibeau lacks honor."

"Melissa, once we get the repairs underway, I want to arrange shore leave for my crew."

"Of course, Jacques." Her grim tone was gone and she smiled radiantly. "I would not hesitate to offer your crew some well-deserved leave. Nor would I deny my merchants of the customers."

* * *

"The first convoys of freighters have reached the smelters and shipyards, my Lady."

"Excellent. I knew the citizens of House Tessier would prove more pragmatic than their leader." He troops had seized the former Tessier colony on Maraselle with little effort and minimal bloodshed. "Is output from the mines increasing?"

"Current output is reported to be thirty per cent of pre-annexation levels."

She frowned. "Thirty per cent?"

"Yes. Some of the mines on Maraselle were damaged by the bombardment. Transportation hubs were also damaged and require repairs. It will take time to get the colony fully integrated with our other holdings."

She sighed. "I suppose I can spare a little time. But no slacking! I want the mines' output back to normal levels as quickly as possible." Her growing military needed more raw materials to continue expanding. "What word of the missing courier ships?" Logs reported that there should have been nearly a dozen high-speed courier ships docked on the colony. Her troops had seized eight during the annexation.

"Some of the sensor readings are still being examined, but it appears that two or three ships *might* have launched during the battle."

"Find out."

Ryan nodded.

"You have the most advanced ship in the entire Freehold! Surely you can determine if any vessels were present during the battle."

"The asteroid cluster makes readings difficult. Debris from the battle, as well chunks of rock, clutter our sensors. We have patrols watching the trade routes for any couriers." He had taken precautions against word spreading by scattering patrols along the shortest and most commonly-traveled routes between Maraselle and Cadixia.

"We have yet to find Lord Tessier," Yvonne complained.

"I have reports that he is currently on Arcadion."

"Not even present when I attacked? A pity." Matters would have been easier if the fool had been killed.

"My Lady, matters are in hand."

"They had better be." She swirled the wine in her glass. "We are now entering previously uncharted territory. We risk everything...but my House could win the ultimate prize!" She laughed and drained her glass.

* * *

"I was surprised to see non-Simard ships docked with the station."

"We have to trade with other Houses to get some goods. I'm sure LaLonde trades with its rivals as well." Every House conducted widespread trade, even as their militaries clashed over control of the system's resources. "No House can afford to stand alone." *A fact of life.*

"I'm sure some of them would like too." Devin stepped closer to the railing. The balcony overlooked a stretch of the multi-level bazarre. Located near the station's central core, the shopping district was a large open space—a vital illusion of openness for humans who spent most of their time in cramped starships.

"It's not as vibrant as the shopping boulevards in Arcadion, but not bad either. The prices tend to be reasonable too." Jacques pointed to a tavern a few hundred meters away. "That is a good bar."

"You buying?"

"No, you can." Jacques chuckled. "The *Jolly Roger* takes credits from all Houses."

1 Chapter Fifteen

"So she just wiped out Lord Tessier and the Maraselle colony?"

"Most of it." Melissia still sounded horrified.

Jacques shook his head in stunned wonder as he leaned back in his chair. "How could she have committed such an act?" he said aloud. Tessier had controlled one of the numerous asteroid clusters; his House capitol had been a particularly large asteroid—almost large enough to be considered a planet.

"She's insane." Melissia had poured them all drinks before sharing the grim report she had just received via courier. "She bombarded the surface from orbit and breached the domes."

"That violates the rules of engagement." Devin was shocked. *How could she do that?*

"Some of the interior caverns must have survived. It's likely Thibeau landed troops to secure the holdings for herself."

"More territory for her House. At the cost of how many lives?"

"Too many."

Devin shook his head in bitter disbelief . "Didn't we lose enough after the Exile?" he demanded. "Didn't we see everything fall apart?"

"Our ancestors brought us here. They settled this world."

"And they started a war that almost destroyed Cadixia. They could have wiped out every living thing on this world and where would that have left our people?"

"We have rebuilt." Melissa watched the two officers stare at each other, noting how alike they were. *I can see why Jacques likes him.* "It took us over a millennium before our ancestors were able to reach orbit, let alone explore the rest of this system."

"Yes," Devin agreed, "and the Lords are still fighting over the resources here. Our people are trapped within a cycle of violence and hate."

"We have no choice," Jacques pointed out. "The cycle of the Resource Wars dominates our lives. How can we break the cycle?"

"We have to break it!"

"I agree with the LaLonder."

"You do?"

"If we do not end the Wars, we will not survive as a people. We will be lucky to survive as a species."

* * *

"A most impressive design, is it not, Marcel?"

Lord Chenier nodded as he looked around the command deck. "Your new toy is certainly different to the usual designs," he agreed. "It's not from any shipyard I know of."

"No, it was christened and launched from *Arcadia* before the Exile."

Chernier's eyes widened. "You're joking."

Yvonne laughed lightly. "No, it truly is that old. My House found it at one of our mining colonies. We've refurbished it and now the *Jeweled Gauntlet* will carry me to victory."

"I see."

"You do not sound impressed."

"I am impressed," he told her, "and more than a little nervous. This ship is a powerful weapon...in both military and symbolic terms. You command a ship that carried our ancestors to this star system. That fact alone will give your ideas and statements weight with the common citizens of all Houses. You could use it to set yourself in power as First Lord."

"I plan to do so."

His eyes narrowed. "By declaring war on the other Houses?"

"I have the firepower."

"You are only *one* House."

"I have allies." She looked sharply at him. "Don't I?"

He heard the danger in her voice. "Of course you do, Lady Thibeau." He paused, licking his lips nervously. "But whether it is enough to dominate the others...."

"Do you question my resolve?"

"Never."

"Then you will support me?"

"Yes..." *Though you leave me little choice.*

"Excellent. I knew you would see things my way." Yvonne gestured grandly to her crew. "Helm, set our course for Cadixia. Best speed."

"As you command." The captain bowed. "I will signal the fleet."

Chenier watched the officer begin issuing orders to the crew. "My Lady," he began, "why Cadixia?"

"It is the key to the Freeholds."

Marcel frowned. "Word is already spreading about your seizure of Maraselle."

She grimaced. "The fools who let those couriers escape have already been punished."

"Surely this is a time for caution then. Why risk war when negotiation could net you the Freeholds? You have the firepower to bargain from a position of obvious strength."

"Bargaining is not going to end the Resource Wars!" she snapped. "We must deal with the traitors in Arcadion. By striking at their head, we can destroy the other Houses before they can hope to unify against us. The survivors will fall into line with us easily enough. This is our one chance to avert what might become a nasty war."

"Yvonne, you cannot attack that world!"

"My forces are already heading towards it. The first elements should be within strike range in an hour or so."

He stared at her. "You're mad."

"Am I?" Yvonne smiled sweetly. "Is it *madness*, or *greatness*?" she demanded. "If I succeed, future generations will praise me as the Savior of Cadixia!"

"If you fail," Marcel countered grimly, "those same future generations will curse your name." *Assuming that anyone survives this insanity.*

1 Chapter Sixteen

"...and tell that Chenier flotilla to shift their vectors. They're drifting off-course."

"Yes, Admiral."

"The Thibeau flotilla is closing."

Morgan Davidson shook his head. "As if space around here isn't crowded enough." Freighters and liners made constant runs to and from Cadixia and the rest of the Freeholds. *And I get the pleasure of keeping them in order...a lost cause most of the time,* he thought grimly as he paced towards the bank of sensor displays. *Traffic control for the most important planet in the system. Why did I get chosen?* Luck the draw or did some political enemy have it in for him? "Order Thibeau to slow their approach to normal speeds." *What's their hurry?*

"House Tessier is issuing a protest at the approach of Thibeau."

"Comm, inform Tessier that Cadixia is neutral space and open to everyone. Remind Tessier that Station Prime is a neutral open port and will enforce its neutrality by force if necessary. Remind Thibeau of that fact as well," he added grimly.

"Aye, Sir."

Why do I put up with this crew? he wondered. It was a delicate job to juggle the conflicting loyalties of everyone onboard the station. Supposedly the crew members foreswore their House allegiances for the duration of their duties onboard. *In theory having personnel from every House should act to keep the rivalries to a minimum.* In practice.... He grunted.

"The Thibeau flotilla has passed the main picket lines...now entering standard traffic lanes."

"Send them a beacon. Give them a parking vector."

"Transmitting now."

That looks like more signals than we were expecting. Morgan eyed the displays of his command center and frowned. He signaled his aide. "How many ships are coming in?"

"According to today's schedule?"

"Yes, Alex."

"Civilian traffic should see forty-five freighters depart from Cadixia and another thirty-two enter orbit. Liner traffic is limited to seven ships departing and three incoming." Alex checked the small note-puter in his hand. "Mostly LaLonde and Simard liners leaving; three and four respectively. Two LaLonde and one Graham liner incoming."

Morgan nodded. "And the military hulls?"

"Five from Graham, two from LaLonde, fifteen from Thibeau, and seven from Simard."

Morgan's eyes narrowed in suspicion. "There are more than fifteen vessels in Thibeau's flotilla." Easily three times that many according to the latest sensor scans. *Added to the two dozen or so ships already in orbit, that gives her House a considerable fleet.* He didn't like it. *This must be more than just a simple gathering of resources. That bitch is up to something.* "Signal Thibeau to cut her speed and hold her current position."

"On what grounds?"

"On the grounds that I don't like her having that many ships in orbit of this planet." *Not after she attacked Maraselle.* But then he gave himself a quick mental shake. *Not even she would dare fire on Cadixia. This world is inviolate.*

"Transmitting now."

"Alex, signal our *Stiletto* pilots to stand by for launch."

"Yes, Sir." Alex eyed the display. "Are you expecting an attack?" he asked. There were no obvious targets within range. No ships were moving along obvious attack vectors. *There are so many signals in orbit...keeping track of them all during a battle will be a nightmare.*

"I'm not sure what I'm expecting. I do know that Thibeau leveled Maraselle with a massive assault and I don't like her showing up here with three times the ships she claimed were coming." Cadixia was an important world to all the Houses, but even so....

"The other stations are watching."

"I know that." Station Prime was merely the largest structure in planetary orbit. Most of the other Houses maintained space-bourn facilities of their own for cargo transfers and to maintain a watch on the comings and goings of their rivals. Then there were the communications satellites and astronomical observatories, deep-space relays, commericial tugs, and myriad other artificial objects.

"Thibeau is not acknowledging our instructions."

"Warn them again."

"Visual feed from one of our picket fighters. I'll patch it through."

The main display flickered.

"Look at the size of that ship!" someone cried out.

"I don't recognize the design." Morgan Davidson shook his head as he studied the massive vessel. The other ships were just standard brigantine and cruiser designs, but the flagship was completely unknown to him. "Run it through the database."

"At once."

"Comm, warn it off." He didn't want it getting any closer to Station Prime then it already was.

"It's got Thibeau markings."

"That damned woman again."

"It's coming towards us, Admiral." Alex made that observation in a formal tone-of-voice. "Approaching weapons' range. They are not responding to our hails."

Morgan nodded calmly. *No choice then.* "Open fire. Repeat, all guns open fire!"

"We're coming under fire from Station Prime."

Major Coleman nodded his acknowledgement of the report. "Circle about, flank the Station and try to stay out of its range."

"Why worry, Major?" Yvonne called out from the observation deck. "Your weaponry has superior range. Take advantage of it."

"We have mobility as well, but I don't relish closing with the Station." He shook his head as he considered the schematics and sensor readings. It was a huge construction, bristling with massive amounts of firepower. "It will take some time for us to breach its defenses."

"You have a fleet."

"With weaponry requiring them to engage from within the station's own range. Our escorts will be ripped to shreds."

"We can afford some losses to secure the planet."

"Yes, my Lady."

"Do I need to make this an order, Major?"

"I merely point out that the Station is immobile. There are numerous warships in the area which I consider to be more of a threat."

"Station Prime could become a stronghold against our control of the orbital lanes."

"With all due respect, my Lady, you are not a military strategist."

Yvonne stared at him, unused to being so bluntly addressed.

"This is now a battlefield," Ryan pressed on. "One needs to know the strengths and weaknesses of one's opponents. Station Prime is a threat, but only to a limited area of space. The mobile assets of our rival Houses are considerably more dangerous and must be neutralized before we can move to secure orbit."

Yvonne nodded reluctantly. "I leave the battle in your hands then, Major. Do not fail me."

1 Chapter Seventeen

"Move out, we've got to secure that communication station."

"Look out!"

Bullets shattered the windows in the office tower they were passing.

"House Simard." Danielle Nystul squeezed off a long burst from her Sirocco rifle. As the rest of her squad sought cover, they began firing their own weaponry at whatever targets they could see. "Control, this is Strike Beta. We're short of the target and under fire from Simard units."

A fresh chatter of gunfire erupted to the west.

"*Strike Beta, this is Gamma. We've encountered Simard units here as well.*"

"*This is Alpha...engage at will.*"

"Beta Lead here, where did the Simards come from?" Danielle adjusted her comm-encryptions to ensure the conversation remained private. "This was supposed to be a cake-walk."

"*This is the capitol city...some interference was anticipated.*"

"After we secured Arcadion, Alpha. Not before."

"*Continue to advance on target. Alpha out.*"

* * *

"Lord Karul!"

Nicholaus turned from watercolor he was painting. "Yes?" he asked calmly. The moment of creation was on him.

"A Thibeau fleet is firing on Station Prime."

The paintbrush dropped from his fingers to splatter the wood paneled floor. "*Thibeau?*" His tone was thick with disbelief. "Attacking Station Prime?" He shook his head. "What does she hope to accomplish?" he demanded.

"I don't know."

"Jules, get me update information." He hurried towards his office, abandoning his painting. "Patch me through to the planetary grid."

"Yes, my Lord."

"I *must* find out what is happening." *A limited strike*, he told himself. *She wouldn't risk more than that.*

* * *

"Incoming missiles!"

"Point defense is clear to engage." Martin Reeve felt the *Sheath*-class *Vainglorious* shudder as two missiles struck the outer hull and exploded. "Return fire, all batteries!" A House Graham cruiser was pulling away, trying to escape before the larger warship could pound it back.

Near-Cadixia orbit was a mess. Warship patrols from every House were routinely placed in close parking orbits, or else passing past rival Houses as they sought surface landings. Normally they ignored each other, or else simply traded volleys of insults. Now, the Houses were actively engaged in firing upon each other.

"Any further signals from Lord Bouchard?" Martin demanded.

"No, Captain. The capitol has gone silent."

"Impossible." He rounded on the other officer. "How could you lose contact with the capitol?"

Captain Gavin Douglas shrugged helplessly. "It's chaotic down there right now. Jamming on most frequencies. Power interruptions. I'm picking up short-range signals...reports of street fighting and riots. The planet has gone mad!"

"It was Thibeau! She did this."

"She has allies. Graham hit us. Chenier has opened fire on a LaLonde starbase."

"Madness." Martin shook his head in horror.

* * *

Jonathan LaLonde grabbed at the edge of his chair as the deck-plates shook.

"Hull breached, cargo section."

"My Lord, you should be seeking shelter."

"My place is here, Robert." He gestured to the command center where dozens of technicians bent over their consoles in intense concentration. "If my station is under attack, then I should be here." His blue eyes flicked across the displays. *If the station is boarded where will I be safer than in central command?* Or if the station was simply destroyed by weapons' fire, where he was taking shelter wouldn't matter. "How bad are the odds?"

"So far two patrols of Chenier ships. Full fighter complements on them both. The patrols seem to be content, so far, in trading missile fire with us." *A futile effort that. This station has considerably more missiles stored in its magazines than those warships could carry.*

"Point defense?"

"Active. Our own *Stilettos* are engaged and holding off the bulk of the enemy fighters."

"Warships?"

"Still engaged in battle around Cadixia."

Jonathan eyed the displays showing that battle. The time-lag was minimal, with events shown being only a few minutes old. The battle had spread across the entire globe, as ships attempted to out-manouever their rivals or make flanking attacks. "What is Thibeau trying to do?"

"She is trying to secure power for herself." Robert paused as tactical called for point defense to engage an incoming volley of missiles. "Chenier is just trying to settle an old grudge."

"He picked a fine time for it." *Has he allied himself with Thibeau then? Or merely taking advantage of the confusion to deal with me?* "Can we contact the other Lords? Surely the others are fighting back."

"The situation is confused right now, my Lord." Robert gestured to one display. "Every House in orbit is fighting with at least one other rival. We can't even tell who is allied with who at this point. It looks like a free-for-all."

"Chaos."

"Disaster more like."

Jonathan shook his head. "Defend the station, Robert, that's all I can ask of you."

"I will not fail you, Lord."

* * *

"Fighting has broken out on Cadixia."

"What?" Devin looked up from his drink. "Fighting?"

The other officers at the table stared at the captain. The cards in their hands were forgotten as they tried to make sense of Jacques's words. He had just burst into the officer's lounge and announced that warships were battling over Cadixia.

"Word just came in over the comms. Thibeau strike troops struck at a dozen targets in the capitol city yesterday. Almost without opposition. They took control of the main power generation station, as well as two military depots. One from Tessier and one from Bouchard."

Devin shook his head. "That's insane."

"Are you sure this is a real report?"

"As much as we can be, Erik." Jacques shook his head. "The Comm section is intercepting messages on all House frequencies. Most of them aren't even coded." Which was very unusual—every House encoded even routine updates to prevent their rivals from learning too many secrets. "Too many of them are cutting off in mid-word. Right now there's reports of street fighting in a dozen locations around Arcadion. Thibeau started it, but the other Lords are defending their own territory with every soldier they can muster. It's not a pretty sight."

Devin shook his head grimly. "The capitol is too divided." *Each House controlled a portion of the city...now those distinctive neighborhoods were becoming battlefields.* "What has possessed Lady Thibeau to do this?"

"That's the question of the hour."

"Are we going there?"

"I have already set the course. We're heading there at full speed. I gave Engineering strict instructions to push the engines." No doubt every House would be recalling ships to Cadixia. Given the communication delays between the far-flung Freeholds, every Lord would want to be present at the scene of the battle, and no one would wish to see control of Cadixia fall to any single House.

"It's going to take us a while."

"You have time to get the ship combat-worthy. I want all the fighters fuelled and armed. Weapon systems will ready for battle." He gestured to the table. "You should still have time to finish your card game though."

"Who can concentrate on cards now?" Erik asked scornfully.

"We have civilians in danger."

"We have a real war on our hands." Devin closed his eyes. "How could this happen?"

1 Chapter Eighteen

"There is significant fighting reported throughout the Freehold. You have done the unthinkable, Lady Thibeau, and provoked a full-scale war."

"I have done what needed to be done in order to ensure the survival and prospering of the Cadixian People." She glared at her supposed allies. "You all command holdings for my House. There is no point in trying to stop what has been done."

"Lady, the damage done to the capitol is already extensive. Surely you cannot desire to see the entire city reduced to rubble."

"Governor Duval, I am willing to take whatever action is necessary to end the Resource Wars. If that means destroying this city, then so be it."

The coldness in her voice made the nobles look nervously at each other.

"I rule this House and its holdings. If you do not wish to obey my commands, you are more than welcome to step down and I will find more suitable replacements for your positions." She stared across the lounge. Francois Station was fully operational and the current battle lines were far enough away that it could be considered safe.

"We are merely interested in seeing an end of the fighting. The slaughter of innocents will not serve our cause."

"You have brought significant numbers of warships to the capitol," Yvonne reminded them. "The full strength of House Thibeau has been mobilized. Our hidden assets are now on display. The other Houses cannot stand against us."

"You claim a victory then?"

"I present that possibility." She smiled. "Our time is now!"

* * *

"Cut power to engines, let us drift." Neil Latimer gripped the sides of his chair. "We don't want to be spotted."

"I hardly think that's likely, Captain. There's so much junk around here, no sensor could pick us out of the debris."

"You had better keep telling yourself that, Mitchell." After another moment glaring at his helm officer, Neil shifted his blue eyes towards the bridge displays. "If one of those Simard ships spots us, we're dead." His freighter had been heavily modified when it had been assigned to courier duty. Larger engines for faster speed and additional weaponry for defense...but those modifications would not be enough to fend off a full Simard patrol if the *Evening Breeze* was detected.

"What was so bloody important that we had to come to Tigress?"

"A pick-up we had to make." Neil frowned. "I think they're passing by." The patrol was moving deeper into the asteroid cluster.

"I don't think they got a sharp sensor lock."

"Lucky for us."

"Captain, the patrol is recalling its fighters."

"Let them clear sensor range, then boost us away from their last known vector."

"Destination?"

"Asteroid Tigress Five-Nineteen."

"That's a small port. Barely a refueling depot."

"We have a passenger waiting for us."

"He had better be bloody important."

"Mitchell?"

"We're in hostile space, Captain. During a war."

"I know the risks. We will serve as our Lady commands."

"Yes, Captain."

* * *

"Coming in hard and fast." Georges Sharplen checked his flight readings as the twenty meter long *Dagger*-class fighter-bomber dove out of the clouds. "Target coming up ahead...stand by." He checked his vector and speed. *Right on schedule.* "Weapons hot, Ian."

The gunner checked his own displays. "Launchers loaded. Reloads are primed and ready."

Georges smiled, expression hidden behind his visor. "Then it's time to light some candles." *And we've got two launchers with fifteen missiles apiece ready to launch.* They were limited-yield warheads of course, designed for explosive power but nothing else. *No exotic warheads on this run.*

The fighter's comm-system crackled. "*You are approaching the designated target, Talon Lead. We've got the locals tied up. Clear to engage at will.*"

"Copy that, Flame Lead." *Glad I'm not out there mixing it up with the local* Stiletto *fighters,* he thought. *I much prefer to simply hit and run from my targets...a sustained dogfight is just asking to get yourself shot down.* His *Dagger's* missiles were armed, their warheads ready. The other five fighters of his flight were in a loose wedge, flanking him. "Fire!" he shouted into the comm as the military base came into visual range.

"*Birds away!*" Ian called out.

Explosions erupted behind him.

"*Major damage to the airfield,*" one of his pilots radioed.

"I'm taking us back around for another pass...lasers ready." General Lucien Thibeau had ordered the local defense forces be neutralized before their ground troops could begin seizing other cities. *An order I will happily obey.* He adjusted his speed, slowing for this second run. Smoke was rising from numerous locations. "Looks like we took out the main anti-aircraft defenses." Good, it would limit potential losses for these follow-up runs. "Fire on any and all targets of opportunity."

"*Copy that, Lead.*"

* * *

Fires were burning freely in the suburb.

A dull thump sounded as a *Trebuchet* lobbed a shell from its main turret. The tank shifted slightly on its treads and fired again.

Ewan Gosling winced as flames exploded from the upper floors of an apartment tower. "This is not right," he muttered. *Even if this is Thibeau territory, we should not be razing every building in sight.* But Lord Bouchard had ordered no mercy, and he had to obey the ruler of his House.

"Captain, we have reports of Trembley troops advancing on the eastern flank. Two squads with armored support moving towards the Rosewater Canal."

"Divert Lieutenant Jager to halt their advance at the Diamond Bridge."

"Yes, Captain."

"Contact Control and request reinforcements. I can't continue to expand our perimeter if I have to divert my troops to fight off other Houses." City fighting was more confusing than he had ever anticipated. *None of us ever practiced for this madness. We never expected to see battle in the streets of the capitol!*

* * *

"The blockade is most effective so far. Our House has secured the orbital lanes and is preventing the other Houses from landing reinforcements on Cadixia."

"Yes, my Lady."

"I was confident in the superiority of our pilots' training. Our fighter screens have prevented any other House from approaching orbit."

Lucien Thibeau shook his head. "True, my Lady, but we are in tying down a significant number of our own ships in this blockade. There is fighting elsewhere in the system."

"Control of one world will not win the war," another officer pointed out.

"But control of *this* world will!" Yvonne countered. "Cadixia is the key to the Freeholds."

The officers nodded reluctantly.

"The battle is now at an ebb. My fighter escort was not bothered in the slightest by any other attacks."

"There was a fierce engagement being fought to the south of the city. Simard sought to sink several of our transport barges as they approached the city. The fighting quickly spread as Graham and Chenier got involved with Bouchard. We are still tallying the losses to all involved."

"I saw the fighting from orbit as we descended. The damage is widespread." Her tone mingled dismay with sadness.

"The fighting spread more quickly than we had originally anticipated. Most of our attempted surgical strikes failed to achieve their goals. The other Houses were more quick to deploy armed troops than we thought." Lucien frowned. "You should not have come down here, Yvonne. You were safer in orbit."

Ian Keating quickly nodded his agreement. "The city is not secure."

"I trust you and your men, Commander." She smiled at him. "This neighborhood is ours. House Thibeau has controlled it for centuries." *Since the founding of Arcadion.* "If I cannot be safe here on the island, then where will I be safe?"

"I shall do my best, my Lady." Ian bowed to her. Thibeau's holdings were on a veritable island. Wide and deep canals acted as a potent line of defense around the neighborhoods loyal to his House. With well-placed strong points, his troops could engage anyone attempting to cross the canals via the bridges or by boat. *And we have many strong points already established. I can hold this part of the city.*

"In the meantime," Lucien said, "we should seek shelter immediately. Standing here invites sniper attack."

"Surely we are out of range."

"With so much open fighting along the borders, as well as scattered riots, I cannot be certain that no malcontents or House agents have infiltrated into this region." Ian sounded apologetic. "I am diverting additional patrols to maintain security, but right now the situation is volatile." He shrugged. "I don't have the strength I need to maintain optimum security. The perimeter is taking every soldier I can muster."

"I see." A squadron of *Stilettos* soared past, heading northward. "Let us adjourn to the war-room then. I wish to be fully updated on the situation." Full battle reports were not being broadcast on open frequencies.

"Yes, this way, my Lady."

1 Chapter Nineteen

"Shipping units are closing."

Jacqueline Delaportas checked her displays, but the fighter was operating normally. "Any sign of our target?"

"You should be coming up on it, Flight Leader."

"Copy that." A sensor chimed. "I see it."

"Hard to miss it," one of her fellow pilots radioed. *"One big freighter out in the middle of the ocean."*

"One big target." Jacqueline adjusted her speed. "We have our orders. That vessel is to be *sunk.*" Simple orders from the High Command: cut off the flow of supplies to the capitol and force the other Houses to either capitulate or starve. *Doesn't matter to me which they choose.*

"Copy that."

"Break and attack. Weapons hot." One pass with the lasers should punch enough holes in the hull to sink the freighter. "Going in."

"New signals, Leader. Incoming aircraft."

"Transponders?"

"Looks like Tessier."

"Warn them off. If they keep closing, shoot them down." The freighter was lumbering through the water, its wake churning the waves.

"I've got a missile lock!"

"Confirm that?"

"Going evasive. Going evasive!"

Jacqueline raked the freighter with her lasers. Smoke rose from several of the hits, but it didn't look like she had hit anything vital in her first pass. "Report Two." There was silence from the comm. "Report, Two."

"Two bought it, Leader. I'm taking fire. Three Tessier Stilettos."

"I'm coming up." She checked her displays. *Damn.*

* * *

The Park of Ever-Singing Nightingales was momentarily quiet.

Danielle cursed as bullets snapped past her head. "Push on here," she snapped into her radio. "We're pinned down. I need support."

"There is none currently available."

"I need Armour support."

"There is none available," the officer on the other end of the comm replied.

"Why not?" She snapped off a short in the direction of the enemy. Whether she hit anyone was a pure guess of course.

"House LaLonde forces are pushing towards the Bridge of Golden Sparkles...Tremblay units are advancing on our forward positions as well. All units are committed to holding the Bridge."

"I can't hold the Park with just my squad."

"Do what you can."

"Damn it! I need support!" Danielle crawled towards a broken statue. The pedastal would give her some cover.

* * *

"Anything new from the planet?"

"It's confusion down there. Plain and simple."

"It's not much better organized up here."

Martin Reeve winced as a brief-lived explosion destroyed one of the House Bouchard cruisers leading his patrol into battle. "What type of weaponry is that monster armed with?" he demanded. The Thibeau vessel was proving extremely dangerous to approach as it maintained a geosynchronous orbit directly over Arcadion.

"A particle beam, we think. It's got better range than we do."

"Do we launch another attack?

"What else can we do?" Martin asked. "Lord Bouchard has demanded that we beak the blockade and provide his troops with reconnaissance information." Most of the communication and observation satellites in Cadixian orbit had been destroyed within the first day of Thibeau's assault. Replacements were being destroyed almost as quickly as they were launched.

"Houses Chenier and LaLonde are exchanging fire near the moon."

"Who are we allied with?" *At this point in the battle, I have no idea,* Martin admitted to himself. The web of ever-shifting alliances was getting even more confused.

"LaLonde, I think."

"They're on their own for now. We need to try and take down that monster."

"Yes, Captain."

* * *

"I want a quick strike at the target." Yvonne gestured to the city map. "It is a military complex, and thus a valid target."

Lucien licked his lips. "My Lady, I am not sure about this."

"What troubles you, Uncle?"

Your sanity, I think. "The complex is located close to a residential area of the city. A strike there, if it fails to be precise, will inflict considerable damage."

"I am willing to take a risk, General." Yvonne tapped the map. "A strike there will eliminate Lord Karul and eliminate one rival to the title of Lord of Lords. That will rally our allies and dishearten our foes. Arrange for the attack at once."

"Aerial defenses are powerful around that complex." Each House had its military command center heavily armed and well-defended. "Any air strike will be costly."

"Use the ground troops to distract them. Let Karul believe the fighters are merely providing support for a push by our troops towards his command center. Then when the *Daggers* hit, he'll be taken by surprise."

"It will be a costly battle for us," Lucien pointed out grimly. "Many of our soldiers will die providing this *distraction* you desire."

"Use the penal brigade then." Soldiers who had been found guilty of crimes, and common civilian criminals, who would be sent into battle under the belief that surviving the battle would earn them a pardon and freedom.

"Yes, my Lady."

"It must be done," she told him. "For the glory of our House."

* * *

Georges Sharplen adjusted the flight vector as his *Dagger* weaved between two office towers. Windows shattered from the force of his passage.

"Damn fool place to fight a battle," his gunner muttered.

"Tell me about it. What is the Old Bat thinking?" Georges could scarcely credit the orders from his Lady. A full-fledged air strike against a target inside city limits? "If we miss the complex, we'll inflict heavy civilian deaths."

"Price of war I guess."

"True, we can rebuild the city later."

Explosions erupted below him as Thibeau ground units exchanged fire with Karul's supporters. Several fires raged uncontrolled.

"We're coming up on the attack point. Stand by to break off." Georges watched part of his *Stiletto* escort peel away to engage a flight of Karul *Stilettos*. "Form up," he radioed the rest of his squadron.

One of the Thibeau *Daggers* was hit by anti-aircraft fire and plunged groundward. It crashed into a canal and exploded.

1 Chapter Twenty

Yvonne stood at the huge windows of her office, watching the distant cityscape as it burned. *So much smoke...so much of our history is being lost*, she mused sadly. *Why do the others force me to take these actions? Why can't they accept my rule over them? Stubborn fools...to invite such destruction upon their city and holdings. It will require much effort to rebuild...but the reconstruction will be a good thing. It will help to unite the formerly divided factions. The city will be better in the long-run.*

"My Lady?"

"Yes, Captain?" She turned from the window, gracing him with a smile.

Ian Keating stood at attention. "The most recent battle report indicates our fighters are continuing to take heavy losses, but they *have* disrupted Karul's defense lines. Our *Daggers* are ready to strike."

"They already have their clearance from me. Let them strike and deal with Karul once and for all."

"As you wish." Ian spoke into a handheld communicator. "*Daggers* are cleared to strike." He listened to the acknowledgement.

Yvonne smiled. "The battle is almost over then."

"The price is going to be high, my Lady. Very high."

"The city can be rebuilt."

"And what of the lives lost?" Ian asked quietly. "What of the blood spilled?"

Yvonne gave no sign that she had heard him.

A distant thump rattled the windows.

"So much for the pride of House Karul." Yvonne lifted a jeweled goblet to her lips as a fresh cloud of smoke rose from the east. "Next we shall send our forces to seize the mines on Bijou."

* * *

"Reports are still coming in, but it's not pretty."

Roy Simard gestured to the visuals playing out on the screens. "That bitch attacked Karul's main command center."

Jean-Paul nodded from the monitor conveying his image. "*So I can see.*"

"She has gone too far!"

"*I agree, but what more can we do? We are already at war with her House.*"

"We will do what we can to aid the civilians who survived."

* * *

Karul winced as a medic dabbed at the cut on his face. "Get away from me!" he snapped.

"Your injury requires treatment."

"Others are hurt worse than me. Attend to them." Adjust his torn cloak, Karul pulled himself free of the medics and hurried into the open air.

The breeze carried the stench of burned flesh.

"How bad is it?"

"As bad as it looks." The major was watching a column of soldiers moving through a half-collapsed building. "The air strike hurt us badly." They did not appear to be having much luck at finding survivors.

Karul watched them as well. "I was surprised to see that flight of *Daggers* trying to break though our air cordon." He had never expected those *Daggers* to be sent to target his command complex. "I thought they would try to support the ground push."

"The ground push halted at the Sapphire Bridge. Since the blast, it has collapsed."

"The bridge or the push?"

"Both."

Karul winced. *Even if the war ended right now, it would take years to repair the city and rebuild what has been lost. No title can be worth this much suffering and loss.* "What caused the blast? A bombing run?"

"Sort of." The major shook his head, still trying to grasp what had happened. "The initial bombs caused minor damage to the complex. The attack wasn't really targeted that well. Looked like they were hitting targets of opportunity."

"Trying to break our defenses?"

"Maybe. In any event, one of *Daggers* was shot down by an anti-aircraft tower and smashed into the Sirocco office. The explosion's magnitude is still being calculated." It had leveled every building for four blocks.

"Some new type of bomb?"

"We believe so, Lord."

A most dangerous development indeedt. "Civilian deaths?"

"Very high, Lord."

"That bitch will pay for this." His tone was harsh. "Attacking me within the heart of the city has gone beyond the rules of engagement." She would never be able to make amends for this. "Set up a comm-relay. Inform all commands that I am still alive." Before his troops heard too many rumors and lost morale. "Then order my captains to watch the current borders. Yvonne will not pass up a chance to strike at us while we are *demoralized.*"

"She will expect us to be in a state of confusion?"

"With my death and no clear successor, my House's holdings here in the capitol will be perceived as vulnerable. Yes, she will move quickly to secure an advantage."

"Her troops will not gain another meter."

"That will do...for now." *She will be driven back and exiled from this world!* he vowed. "She will regret this action."

* * *

"Report from our mining outpost at ACT-Beta-Two."

"Yes?" Yvonne stood on her balcony, staring at the battered cityscape. The breeze was blowing from the ocean and the air was clear of smoke. *For a change.* "Continue, General." The boom of artillery echoed.

"Communications have been spotty of late in that area. Several of the long-range transmitters were damaged by saboteurs."

"I *am* aware of that, General."

"Yes, my lady." Lucien took a deep breath. "Patrols from House Simard and Bouchard have attacked the outpost. Our defensive units were defeated and destroyed. No survivors."

"None from the warships?"

"None at all."

Yvonne turned, her face pale. "None at all?" she repeated. "Genocide is simply not Simard's style."

"Nor Bouchard's as a rule." Lucien paused, considering his next words. *But in light of the heavy civilian casualties caused by the air strike, what do you expect?* "Nonetheless, the combined House patrols destroyed every last one of our fighters and warships, including their escape pods. Then they bombarded the asteroid until all surface installations had been leveled. The assault continued until the outpost's fusion reactor went critical."

"Impossible."

"Those are the facts as reported."

"*Impossible!*" she snarled. "No Lord would condone his House to launch such an attack."

Yet you ordered us to do something very similar, my Lady...where does it end? "Both Houses are admitting the attack occurred. They announce this is a punishment for our attack on Karul."

Yvonne's eyes narrowed.

"It stands to reason that these attacks will escalate. The bombing strike has shown our willingness to disregard the rules which have governed the Resource Wars for centuries. The other Houses will move to counter with their disregard. I am afraid of the future...afraid that there will not *be* a future for the Cadian People."

"Leave me."

"Yvonne—"

"Leave me!" she snapped.

"As you command."

* * *

Ryan Coleman shook his head. "How could this happen?" he demanded from his aide as he threw the datapad onto the desk. It clattered across the polished surface and fell onto the floor.

"I am not sure, Sir."

"I want the rest of those *Buster* bombs to be accounted for."

"Yes, Sir." The aide saluted and hurried away.

Ryan stared through the view port at the planet below. Dark rain clouds mingled with smoke to cover the capitol. *We recovered a dozen of those bombs from the* Gauntlet, *he thought grimly. How many has my Lady taken for her own use?* Those powerful bombs were not meant to be used against civilian targets. *I don't care what Lord Entress used them for. I will not see them used against a civilian population.*

"Major, Girard warship patrol closing!"

At least this is a fair enemy to fight. "Power to all guns. Combat speed." Thibeau had established a blockade around Cadixia. The other Houses were constantly trying to breach it. *So far, we have maintained the blockade. But how much longer can we hold?* The Thibeau fleet was not strong enough to fight off every other House if all united against them.

1 Chapter Twenty-One

"We're pushing towards orbit."

"But not fast enough," Devin grumbled.

"No, not fast enough," Jacques agreed. "The orbital vectors are confused with ships right now. Patrols from every House are in orbit and most of them are firing on each other." *The battle has been raging for weeks now...I doubt that anyone can tell who is winning.*

"You have allies, don't you?"

"Yes, but they're not all in agreement with us." Jacques frowned at the sheer madness of it all. "House Lukic has refused to commit his patrol to any attacks launched at my command."

"Dean Lukic governs one of your asteroid colonies?"

"Yes, and he has a small patrol there." Jacque highlighted one set of icons on the display. "Yet he refuses to commit them to my command."

"Could he have sold you out?"

"Possibly." Jacques' voice was harsh. "If he did, he will not live long enough to enjoy the fruits of his treachery."

"Where is LaLonde?"

Several icons blinked.

"Your House has patrols scattered widely." Three patrols were holding station a distance from what was left of Station Prime. Two more patrols were skirmishing with a Thibeau patrol and one patrol appeared to firing on a Chenier space station.

* * *

Marcel DesRoches fired a spray of bullets towards the far side of the park. He ducked down to reload his machine gun.

Return fire chipped bits of stone from the coping of the fountain. Water gurgled from half-choked pipes, no longer arcing in graceful jets.

"Too many enemy units in the area."

"We have to hold," he told the voice. People had been chattering over the comm-net during the battle. The park was a wasteland now, after weeks of fighting. Artillery had cratered the grass and tank treads had churned the gravel paths. The air was heavy with the stench of days' old fires.

Artillery shells on the far side of the park. Dirt fountained into the air and fell back to the ground.

Marcel had no idea which side had fired them. He hunkered down behind the fountain and offered a quick prayer.

Screams echoed in the silence left by the explosions.

* * *

Dennis Simard watched silently as the line of citizens filed into the shelter to receive a meager ration of food. His House troops stood watching, to maintain order and prevent looting. The House Lord felt out-of-place in his clean shirt and cloak.

"It has come to this."

Dennis turned. "Yes, it has."

"Our people suffer."

"How can we bring them relief? The roads into the city are held by rival Houses. Food shipments have been disrupted." *Everything has been disrupted!*

"I would suggest air flights or shuttles, but the skies are as much a war zone as the ground."

"Worse than the ground. Life expectancy amongst pilots is down to minutes now." Too many anti-aircraft defenses around the city. *After the assault on Karul, every aircraft is viewed as a distinct threat.*

One of the soldiers approached. "This area is not safe for you, my Lord." He was scanning the area constantly.

"My people are here. I must be here." The city was quiet at the moment, with no artillery duels or significant battles being fought. A rare moment of peace, Dennis thought.

* * *

"*Thunderbolt, you are cleared to proceed. Good luck.*"

Hanse Douglas nodded to himself. "You heard the admiral. Break formation." His brigantine broke away from its fellows and rapidly accelerated towards Arcadion.

"Looks like we're clear," Damian reported from the sensor station. "They're still trading shots with the rest of the patrol."

"Maybe they think we're wounded too badly to keep fighting." *Thunderbolt* had taken several hits during the earlier stages of the skirmish, but most flight systems were still operational.

"We can hope so."

"Head for the surface, best speed."

"Scanning the area for enemy patrols."

"No sign of enemy patrols so far?"

"None, Captain."

"Good, maybe we can slip through the blockade."

* * *

"This is Rogue-One to *Katana*, heading out." Devin triggered his fighter's thrusters and felt the surge of acceleration push him into his chair. *Yes, this is what I live for!*

"*Rogue-One, this is Katana-One. Good luck.*"

Devin smiled. *Even with the static, I can hear his concern.* "Don't worry, One, I'll be home by bed-time."

"*See that you are, Rogue.*"

Laughing, Devin changed frequencies. "Rogue-One to Rogue Flight. Form up on my wing. We're going in hard and fast."

"*Copy that.*"

Devin felt a bit nervous. After all, he was leading a squadron of Simard pilots into one of the most confusing, multi-sided battles in history. *I hope none of them forget that I'm on their side.* It would be embarrassing.

"*Target sighted, Flight Commander.*"

"I see it." A Simard freighter was being harassed by enemy fighters. "Weapons hot." The freighter was already damaged, with atmosphere leaking from its hull.

"*Looks like Thibeau with Chernier support.*"

"Copy that, Three. Thibeau is priority target." The obvious aggressor in this bitter war. "Take them out first." He checked his missiles. "Adders are cleared to fire."

The Simard squadron dove into the dogfight. Their missiles streaked from their launchers.

"*I've got a lock.*"

"*So do I.*"

"*I'm being targeted!*"

"*Six, break hard!*"

"*Rogue-Four, I'm hit!*"

"*Six, respond.*"

Devin winced as he took a quick glance at the display. *I've lost three men!* Thibeau had lost half a dozen and two Chenier fighters were gone as well.

"*Incoming fire!*" someone warned.

Fresh missiles stabbed into the swirling *Stilettos*.

"Where'd they come from?" Devin demanded.

"*LaLonde fighters.*"

"Oh crap." Devin flipped his fighter end-over-end. His sensors screamed out warnings about targeting locks but he stabbed his fingers at the comm-system. "Break off, LaLonde flight. Simard is friendly. Repeat, Simard is friendly."

A laser burned through his wing. His fighter lurched as vaporizing metal knocked him off-balance. Alarms howled.

One of the LaLonde fighters shot past, close enough for him to read the squadron insignia on its fuselage.

Emerald Flight. Devin's eyes narrowed. *Emerald Leader.*

* * *

"We're still unable to achieve orbit."

"I am aware of that." Jacques stared at the displays with tired eyes. "Are all of the freighters here yet?"

"Every freighter that could reach us, Captain."

Jacques counted them up. "We need to relieve the planet. Our people are starving down there."

"Our Lord is down there."

"Most of our Lords are down there," Devin said as he stepped through the hatch. "Along with millions of civilians."

"Are you all right?" Jacques asked, concern on his face.

"Sure," Devin replied. "Nothing like almost getting killed by my own people." He was still wearing his flight suit, his hair sweaty from being under a helmet.

"I didn't see those LaLonde fighters coming. We were *distracted*."

"I caught part of the firefight. You gave that *Broadsword* a good pasting."

"Almost as good as it gave us. Still, repairs are underway. And I'm glad to you see you back here alive." He gave Devin a hug. "Really glad."

1 Chapter Twenty-Two

Lord Karul turned to face the other Lords. The scar on his face looked worse than it felt, but he appreciated the shock value it gave him. "The death toll has now crested one million lives."

The other Lords winced.

"It is an outrage," Lord LaLonde protested. "This cannot be permitted."

"Damage to the city is staggering," Dennis Simard added. "Every battle shatters the local infrastructure all the more. Thousands of citizens are living without power or water."

"This is war like our ancestors fought." Karul allowed contempt to color his tone. "Bloody and brutal and lacking in all honor."

"Thibeau has gone too far this time."

Dennis Simard nodded in grim-faced agreement. "We cannot permit her actions to go unpunished. Cadixia is vital to *all* of our Houses. She must be stopped."

Karul nodded. "These actions leave us only one option. I truly regret this, but we cannot allow such a blatant cowardly attack to be made against this world." Cadixia was the most valuable world in this system, the only world capable of supporting life. "Arrange for a Freehold-wide transmission. I want everyone to hear my words."

The aide nodded and hurried to adjust a camera pick-up. He nodded to Karul after a short time.

After all, I arranged for this moment well in advance, he thought. *Even before inviting the other Lords to come here and talk. They doubted my offer of simple hospitality, they demanded safeguards—not that I blame them—but these Lords at least came.* Karul stood taller, proud and unbowed despite the pain he felt. "Citizens of the Freehold, hear my words.

"Lady Yvonne Thibeau has recently sought to dominate the Freehold for her own purposes. She has thrown the delicate balance of inter-House politics into chaos. She has sought to assassinate the leaders of her rival Houses through military assault. Though I do not fault her for such ambition," he admitted, "I do find much fault with her *tactics*. Yvonne attempted to destroy the capitol city just to kill a handful of Lords. She has brought open warfare to the crèche of our society.

"This rogue behavior cannot be tolerated.

"After consultation and discussion, the Conclave of Lords has issued this decree." He paused for a long moment. "Lady Yvonne Thibeau is hereby stripped of all rank and privilege. She is denied all rights and claims of friendship and succor. House Thibeau is named renegade. As of this moment, all of its assets are forfeit.

"All loyal Cadians bear witness as justice is done."

* * *

"This is HGS *Bloody Knife* to ACT-Gamma-Five. Respond please."

"This is ACT-Gamma-Five. Good to hear a friendly voice."

"Yes, I can imagine. Word from Cadixia is spreading quickly." Second Lord Stefen Graham smiled as he adjusted his green tunic. "We are here to offer our services in protecting the ore processor."

"That would be much appreciated. Most of our garrison was withdrawn for military strikes. We're operating with only a skeleton defense."

"Isn't that a pity?" Stefen kept the mockery from his voice. "We should be entering orbit within the hour."

"We'll be waiting. ACT out."

Stefen paced across the flag bridge of the *Knife*. "Scan the area for Thibeau patrols." His eyes flicked to a bridge display and studied the icons on it. The *Knife* was accompanied by a standard patrol of three *Broadswords*. An additional half a dozen freighters accompanied his patrol. Each of the *Mules* had been modified of course. At ninety meters in length, a freighter was tiny compared to a warship, but each

Mule was optimized for carrying cargo. *Nineteen thousand tons of it,* Graham thought happily. Their four lasers were totally ineffective in battle, but his *Mules* would prove worth of every credit he had spent purchasing and then modifying them.

"Lord, we are approaching the outer perimeter."

"Have you located the defenders?"

"One patrol of cruisers at bearing five seven mark three one. No *Sheathes* in evidence."

Stefen eyed the displays as they were updated with current sensor data. "I see." The ore processing station was a hollowed-out asteroid at the heart of a small asteroid cluster. *Thibeau has stripped the garrison,* he thought. "No sign of other patrols?"

"None within sensor range."

"Excellent." He smiled a cruel grin. His warships alone could win any battle. *But a battle fought here risks destroying the prizes I want to claim.* "Take us in, attack speed. Launch all fighters."

"Yes, my Lord."

* * *

"Keep pushing." Jacques felt his cruiser shudder as enemy missiles impacted against the outer hull. "We're almost into orbit." *And it's costing us heavily to get this far.*

"*Rogue-One here. Thibeau fighters are pulling back to regroup. I think we can actually reach orbit this time.*"

"You're in charge of the screen, Rogue-One." Jacques tried to keep his tone professional. *He's just a pilot.* "Keep the enemy away from us while we make the last push."

"*Copy that.*" Devin chuckled. "*You're the bigger target after all.*"

* * *

"Simard forces are pressing against the defenders at grid five nine mark four one three."

"Order all available ships to reinforce that area." Ryan Coleman studied a tactical display. "Any sign of movement from the other Houses?"

"No, Major."

"The fools. A concentrated push might be able to split our blockade...a single House attack can be overcome by our local superiority."

"Shall I order the *Gauntlet* into range?"

"Maintain a slow advance, but hold us in reserve for now." He paused. "Order the patrol to target the freighters first...they're easy targets."

"Yes, Major."

* * *

A distant series of explosions marked a fresh border skirmish.

Dennis Simard stared at the wall of monitors. "Too many displays with too little good news," he complained.

"At least we are receiving supplies," Monica pointed out. She had concerned herself more with relief efforts for the civilians, leaving her husband to guide the greater war. *Not that I have not contributed some ideas to the strategy board,* she noted. *My husband does not see every gain to be made.*

"Yes, the space port is taking some artillery fire, but a fighter strike soon scattered it."

Officers and technicians moved through the bunker, gathering near computer banks before moving to other stations to talk and compare notes in quiet voices.

"My Lord?"

Dennis turned around. "Yes?" he began and then he smiled, the expression warm and genuine. "*Jacques*! I'm so glad to see you." He gave his son a fierce hug. "By why are you down here?" he asked. "Aren't you needed in space?"

"The battle is calm for the moment. The Thibeau fleet is trying to regroup. We hurt them with our push." It had been a costly blow, but his ships had made it into orbit near a Simard-held space station and shuttles had launched. They were prepared to fight a defensive war now...and the Thibeau fleet was holding itself out of range of the station's firepower.

"The landing of supplies and fresh troops is going well. We're already reinforcing our borders."

"Our fighter pilots are doing their best to guard the shuttles."

Monica nodded. "Not all of your pilots are in space." She was eying the man standing nervously just behind her son. "That's not one of our pilots." Her dark eyes narrowed.

Jacques nodded. "This is Devin Shaw."

Devin knew his cue. "Flight Commander Devin Shaw." He offered a crisp salute. "Originally of House LaLonde."

Dennis raised an eyebrow. "*LaLonde*?"

"I'm sure there's an interesting story behind his presence?"

"I was taken prisoner by your son," Devin replied bluntly. "Now I fly for him."

Jacques put his arm around Devin's shoulder. "He's with *me* now."

The two older Simards exchanged looks. His mother smiled first and extended her hand. "Welcome to our House, Devin."

* * *

"The Simard fleet made it into orbit?" Yvonne's voice was tight with strain. "I gave orders that no shuttle could be allowed to land."

"*I'm sorry,*" Ryan Coleman said from the comm-screen. Static flickered through his image. "*We fought hard, but our forces are over-committed.*"

"And now reinforcements have reached the surface."

"*Only a handful,*" Lucien Thibeau pointed out from a second screen. "*Our resistance continues.*"

"I do not want resistance. I want victory."

"*We do our best.*"

"Major, you have a powerful warship in orbit. Perhaps you should make better use of its firepower."

Ryan blinked at her, clearly not wanting to give voice to her unspoken command.

Lucien felt no such hesitation. "*No! Major Coleman will* not *be using the* Gauntlet *to bombard the capitol.*"

"It was effective against Maraselle."

"*That was a mistaken tactic. It will not be repeated.*"

Yvonne frowned. "I am not used to being questioned, Uncle."

"*You are not a military genius, my Lady. I am your General for a reason. You should listen to me...or else replace me with someone else.*"

For a moment, Yvonne considered it. "Continue to advise me then," she told him. "The victory of our House is in your hands."

1 Chapter Twenty-Three

Stilettos soared overhead and anti-aircraft guns roared to life. The whine of the jet engines faded.

Devin stepped out of the car and stared up at the blocky building. Two armed sentries stood outside the gate. They were wearing full body armor. *I doubt those are the only guards around. Even in the heart of the LaLonde Enclave, with fighting at the borders no one will take chances.* Taking a deep breath, Devin began to climb the stairs and the sentries took official notice of him. "Flight Commander Shaw." He offered his identification papers.

One of the sentries studied the papers closely while the other watched the street. He gave Devin's flight suit a careful study, then he finally nodded. "Go in."

Devin stepped into the office building. The lobby was a cold place, with bare stonework and a handful of military-themed posters on the walls. *I expected the place to be busier. Surely everyone can't be on the front lines?* A major offensive was being waged against the Thibeau Enclave, but no one would lower their defenses deeper in their heartlands either. *There is no trust to be found here.*

An officer stepped forward. "Captain Patrick Quinn. Can I help you?" he asked.

"Flight Commander Devin Shaw."

The man studied the papers. "These are out-of-date, Commander." He looked at Devin with suspicion.

"I've been out-of-touch, Captain."

"Missing in action, I believe, was how the official report read." The woman's voice was colder than space.

Devin turned. "Jennifer."

"That's *Flight Commander* Sommers to you." She stared at him, as if he was some carbon scoring on her *Stiletto*. "Officially you went missing after the Battle of Grid Fifty-Seven."

"Such an awe-inspiring name for an attempt at freighter hijacking."

"We lost most of our fighters and the *Reliance* was crippled in that raid," Jennifer snarled. "Inquisitor Richesse suspected treason allowed the *Simards* to interfere with our mission." Her eyes narrowed and her voice grew colder. "You were thought lost in action and now we find you here, safe and sound."

"Indeed." The captain eyed him. "Can you explain yourself, Flight Commander?" He placed his hand on his holstered side-arm. "A *Stilleto* could never have brought you here from Grid Fifty-Seven. Not alive at least."

Jennifer's mouth twitched. "The last I saw of you, you were fighting for House Simard."

"You almost shot me down!" Devin snapped.

"Pity I missed."

"He was fighting for Simard?" Patrick asked. Hostility was rising in his voice and in his expression.

"Yes, he was leading one of their fighter squadrons." Jennifer looked at him. "I heard your voice clearly on my comm."

"I was rescued by the *Glorious* after the *Reliance* vanished from my scopes. Rescue by the enemy or simply dying in space was no contest." He would make the same choice, no matter who was offering rescue. "I'm back now."

"I don't care. You can explain it to Richesse. Traitor."

Devin stared at her. "I'm no traitor."

"You deserted your House in a time of war." Captain Quinn sounded disgusted. "By your own admission, you have been consorting with the enemy."

"Thibeau is the enemy, not Simard."

"You should be ashamed of yourself." Quinn snapped his fingers. "Guards!"

"How can you do this?" Devin demanded as marines hurried towards them. "I'm a decorated officer."

"You're under arrest on suspicion of treason."

Jennifer had a cruel smile on her face. "You were a disgrace to the Fleet, Devin. I hope they lock you away somewhere."

"Treason carries a death penalty." Patrick kept his voice cold. "That's all he deserves."

* * *

"My Lady!" Ian Kardow hurried through the doorway into the office as a distant thump shook the building. "My Lady?"

Yvonne stood in front of a floor-to-ceiling window, staring out at Arcadion's cityscape. "Yes?" she asked calmly, without looking away from the scene playing out before her. Smoke rose from hundreds of fires, and fresh explosions were erupting in the buildings around her tower. *The city is pretty when it is burning.*

"It's not safe for you to be here," Ian told her. His uniform was marked with dirt. "I can no longer guarantee the security of this complex. You must take shelter."

"In the basement?"

"That would be the safest place." Another thump shook the tower. "House Bouchard and Simard have us within their range. Our anti-aircraft defenses are being targeted...when they're destroyed, we'll be overwhelmed."

"My pilots will protect us."

"Your remaining squadrons are scattered. I don't think we can protect this place for much longer. The battle for Arcadion is over." His mouth twisted in bitter resignation. "We've lost."

"It is not over!" she snarled.

"It is," he replied coldly. "I can continue to fight—and I will do so for as long as I have soldiers willing to follow my orders—but we have no chance of victory. The tide of battle has turned against us. *You* must escape while you can." He offered her a crisp salute. "We soldiers will give our lives for you."

* * *

A distant boom shook the office building.

"The final push against the Thibeau Enclave is underway."

Devin looked up from the table. It was dull and unpolished, the wood stained with unrecognizable marks. "So can I go and rejoin my unit, Inquisitor Weiss?"

"Certainly not." The black-clad Inquisitor looked astonished by the question. "I have reviewed your entire file. Dominic Richesse had much to write about you after your previous trial."

"I was never on any kind of charges," Devin pointed out.

"Not that time."

Devin snorted. "I'm a fighter pilot. My place is in a cockpit."

Jordan Weiss studied the stack of papers in front of him. "Right now, you have no place. At the least, you were absent without leave. At most, you willingly deserted your command and joined with a rival House, betraying a raid to the enemy."

"That's a lie! I was taken prisoner after the raid went wrong."

"Yet you were confirmed as flying a Simard fighter during a recent battle in orbit."

"I was trying to escort relief freighters into orbit. I was fighting against House Thibeau."

"You admit that you were flying an enemy fighter. Prisoners of war are not generally permitted to fly fighters, Mister Shaw."

"The captain of the *Glorious* and I came to an...*agreement*."

"I see." Jordan shook his head. "It must have been quite an agreement then. One worthy of historical record in the annals of inter-House negotiations. I have a report that you were introduced to Dennis Simard and his wife."

"Yeah." *His spies are really effective right now...a pity they weren't this good with keeping track of the Thibeau schemes.*

"Again, most unusual for a prisoner-of-war."

"I wasn't a prisoner."

"Enough protests from you. This matter is wasting our time."

Devin stared at him silently.

"You are found guilty of the charge of absent without leave. The validity of the other charges of consorting with the enemy and treason are still being determined. You will be taken to a more secure location until that time. A proper military base."

"I protest!"

"Do so. You will have time at your trial." Jordan stood up. "Good day, Ex-Flight Commander."

* * *

"The tide of war has turned against us."

Neil nodded grimly. "We've lost too many ships and now our allies are turning against us."

"This base will remain operational and hidden."

"Can you defend it? I must take your report back to Bonavista."

"My marines and fighter squadrons will give their lives for this facility, but Hidden Hope cannot stand for very long against a full-scale invasion. We're a research facility, not a military fortress."

"I will inform the High Command."

"Hidden Hope is uncharted. Only a handful of people know that we exist."

"Right now, that's your biggest advantage."

l Chapter Twenty-Four

Devin was led into the street, chains securing his wrists and ankles. His flight suit had been replaced by a bright red prison coverall. After weeks in the cells, he felt dejected.

The streets of the enclave were all but deserted. Smoke was hanging over the city and fresh columns were rising from the horizon. The dull thump of distant explosions boomed out steadily.

An armored car was waiting at the bottom of the steps. A personnel carrier was turning the corner, half a dozen armored soldiers escorting it. They all held rifles at the ready, even though the area was supposed to be secure.

"How could you let it come to this?" Devin demanded of his own trio of guards. "Why didn't someone stop that crazy bitch?"

"Shut up." Captain Quinn gestured towards the armored car. He was clearly not taking chances. "Get in. It's a short ride to the main base."

Resigned, Devin stumbled forward, two marines escorting him.

A squadron of *Stilettos* soared overhead. The roar of their engines made the windows in the office blocks rattle.

Explosions erupted in the air as anti-aircraft guns chattered to life.

A second squadron of *Stilettos* screamed in low over the city. One of them was trailing smoke and it collided with the upper floors of an office building. The resulting explosion threw glass and debris into the street.

One marine shrieked as a metal girder transfixed him.

Devin shook his head to try and clear it. He was laying in the street, dazed. *How did I get down here?* he wondered.

An armored marine hauled him to his feet. "Come on." He pushed Devin towards the car.

Patrick Quinn sat up, shaking his head in a daze.

The screaming marine was dead.

Anti-aircraft cannon were firing. Sirens were howling.

Devin was shoved into the back of the car.

Quinn stood up. "Wait" he called out.

The marine slammed the door. "Go!" he shouted and the car lurched into motion.

* * *

"How did it all go so very wrong?" Yvonne mused as she studied a tactical display. Her outposts were either mysteriously going silent or else being publicly destroyed. Pitched battles were erupting throughout the system. *Why can't they see I am only trying to do what is best for them all? Why do they betray me like this?* She paced across the deck, her shoes clicking loudly on the floor. "Driven from the surface of Cadixia itself!"

"Things did not proceed as planned."

Yvonne angrily turned to her uncle. "No, Lucien, they did not." She had been driven from her palace even as artillery shells began to reduce the complex to rubble. *The humiliation of it all! Me, being driven away like a frightened animal. My House will not bear the shame of it!*

"At least you escaped from Arcadion."

"Yes. Ian was most insistent."

"A pity then, that he died delaying Bouchard's new advance into our dwindling Enclave." Lucien's expression was one of disappointment. *Thibeau has lost a fine officer.* To say nothing of the scores of *Stilettos* lost protecting Yvonne's shuttle as it headed spaceward. A distressingly high percentage of escaping shuttles had *not* managed to reach the Thibeau fleet.

"We could level Arcadion from orbit."

For a long moment, Lucien could scarcely credit what he had just heard from his Lady's mouth. "*Level* the city?" he repeated at last. "You can't order such an atrocity!"

"Can't I?" she snarled.

He shook his head. "The crew would never obey such an order. It would violate every treaty and law that we hold dear. Our House would lose all honor forever."

Yvonne looked ready to argue the fact. Finally, her shoulders slumped. "Very well, Uncle."

Lucien suppressed a sigh. "A wise decision, Yvonne." He doubted that she was capable of seeing reason. *If she loses her grip on reality, I will have to move against her.* Not a thought he cared to contemplate. *The survival of our House is all that I can worry about. Will she see reason? Will she accept my choice of tactics? Not that we have any real choice left.* "Now we must turn attention towards the future. We must complete our withdrawal from Cadixia. Fall back to a secure holding and rally our military strength. We'll have to fight defensively until the other Houses weary of this bloodshed and we can return to the previous status quo."

"A defeat?"

"Yes, but with luck it will not cost our House too dearly." Lucien kept his tone light. *I value our House above our ruler...if need be, I will sacrifice her life and my own, to safeguard our House's future.*

She sighed, her firm resolve broken.

"My Lady?"

"Yes, Captain?" She turned with an aura of her previous arrogance. She managed to straighten her posture and even patted at her bedraggled hair. "You have something to report?"

Lucien smiled. *She might slacken around me, but her sense of duty will not allow her to appear less than god-like to her subjects.*

"Patrols from House Simard are closing. Our pickets are engaging, but we can't hold them for long. We have been too diluted. Our forces remain scattered around the planet."

"The blockade has collapsed," Lucien pointed out. "We should abandon that strategy."

"Give the final evacuation order. Set course for *Monet* Station." She would concede her holdings on Cadixia...for now.

"Yes, my Lady."

"Order all remaining ships from ACT-Gamma-Five to rendezvous with us at *Monet*."

"Gamma-Five is no longer responding to our communiqués."

"Since when?"

"Since two days ago."

"Send them a priority signal under my codes. I want to know why they went silent."

"Yes, my Lady."

* * *

"It appears to be a victory."

"Of sorts." Jonathan LaLonde stared at the rubble and shook his head. Armed soldiers stood on guard while rescue crews continued to search through the remains of hangers and repair facilities.

Denis Simard offered a polite smile. "Given the damage to your star port, I am willing to offer you the loan of a portion of mine for relief shuttles to land at."

"Thank you." Jonathan eyed his rival. "That is most thoughtful of you."

"I am sure that you would do the same for me." Denis was certain of no such thing, but the gestured counted. "Rebuilding will be difficult."

"And time-consuming."

"Our Houses must have an understanding."

"Indeed."

A shuttle lifted from a distant part of the field. Its engines roared as it rose ponderously off its landing pad. The main engines ignited and it rocketed into the sky.

"The capitol is safe enough, for the moment. I do not wish to see further fighting erupt."

"You want to secure as much of Thibeau's Enclave as you can, Simard."

Denis shrugged. "So do you, LaLonde." He chuckled and waved his arm to encompass the city. "Right now, half the Lords here are plotting how to best carve up Thibeau's holdings."

"I do not wish to see the civilian population suffer more," Lord Karul said as he walked towards the two Lords. A trio of armored soldiers followed him. "Now is a time for rebuilding, not further fighting."

"There is still fighting to be done," Jonathan pointed out in a calm tone. "That bitch fled off-world. She must be hunted down and brought to justice for her crimes." *Or killed in the process.*

"I am aware of that fact. The skirmishing in orbit has ended." Or at least most of it had. There were a few Thibeau ships, too badly damaged to retreat, still fighting and delaying the other Houses from pursuing. "Her navy is pulling back towards Bonavista." At least, that was the projected course.

"Bonavista? It makes sense. Where else can she go but to her homeworld?"

"She will rally her remaining military assets," Denis agreed.

"A unified effort must be made to bring her to *justice*." Karul made certain to empathsize that last word. "This will not be a massacre."

* * *

"I can't believe you pulled that off."

Jacques smiled. "You're worth the effort." He gave Devin a quick look. *He's lost weight.* He didn't care for the haunted look in Devin's eyes either.

"You infiltrated a marine into a LaLonde base!"

"It was a recruitment office," Jacques pointed out. "Security was light, even with you locked in the basement. Getting Sergeant Adler into place was easy. Getting one of my people into the car was harder."

"And the fighter strike?"

"Wasn't any of my doing. We were going to hijack the car while en route and toss Quinn out at the border. Adler took advantage of a distraction."

"He did a good job. I'll thank him later."

"He has already been promoted."

"This isn't going to go over very well," Devin told him. "Now I'm a real traitor."

"No, you're not!" Jacques held Devin at arm's length. "You were falsely accused. The trial was rigged."

"I can't go back home."

"No, but you can make a new home." Jacques heard the hope in his voice. "I hope you can be happy with me."

"Can you be happy with me?" Devin asked after a moment.

Jacques kissed him.

1 Chapter Twenty-Five

"We have fresh news from ACT-Gamma-Five."

"I thought their transmitter was down."

"Apparently it was disabled by terrorists. The outpost is broadcasting once again."

"And?" Yvonne demanded as she stalked across the floor of the command centre.

"House Graham has seized control of that facility."

"House *Graham*?"

"Yes."

"They are my allies!"

"Apparently they have chosen to side with your enemies."

"Punish them!"

"Our resources are stretched thin at the moment." General Thibeau shook his head. "I cannot spare the ships to retake such a minor ore processing station."

"This is unacceptable!" Yvonne snarled.

"It is a fact of life," Lucien countered. "We have nothing else to throw into the mix. Our fleet assets are shattered. Your war has cost this House greatly. All I can do now is *attempt* to hold Bonavista. I am writing off the rest of our holdings."

* * *

Marcel Chernier eyed the map. "Is this accurate?' he asked, without lifting his eyes from the monitor.

"Yes, Lord."

"Excellent." The map showcased the location of every planet, moon, asteroid, comet, and space station in the system. Icons marked the locations of known House forces, a different color for each House. "Yvonne has been keeping us updated on the placement of her forces?"

"Too the best of our knowledge, this map is accurate." Leon Keating gestured. "I vouch for the accuracy of our own House placements. We are using the data supplied by Lady Thibeau, and many of the garrisons have been verified by our agents."

"Excellent." Marcel took note of several placements. "Dispatch any available elements from our Bonaparte garrison to secure the Gatineau habitats."

"Yes, my Lord."

"House Graham is already striking out, cutting its way free from a doomed alliance." *A wise move for that small House.* "We will secure those additional assets for this House." *Yvonne went too far. The other Houses will not rest until they see her dead and her House in ruins. I will not squander my own resources fighting on her behalf.* Not if taking such actions risked the destruction of his own House as well. *Now it is a matter of preserving my House and increasing its strength as best I can. Yvonne is on her own.*

"Your other orders, Lord?"

"Download all of our data on current Thibeau garrisons and transmit copies to the other Lords."

Leon frowned. "The other Lords?" he repeated. "Are you certain you want to do this?"

"The Conclave made its decision. House Thibeau is going to die." A cruel, though just, fate. "We will encourage the other Lords to destroy Yvonne, leaving us to secure her more valuable holdings for ourselves."

"The secret sites?"

"The hidden bases and shipyards must be seized. With them under control, we can use them to rebuild our House until the time is right for House Chenier to dominate the Freehold."

Leon bowed. "As you wish, my Lord."

"Do not fear, Leon, I have already taken a key lesson to heart from this madness." He shook his head. "When I move to secure the system for my House, it will not be with purely military means." *Yvonne's death will teach us that much.* "Some Houses, at least, will retain their honor."

* * *

"Our allies are continuing to abandon us, my Lady."

"So I observe." Chernier would pay dearly for his betrayal. *I will see my House rise from this defeat and I will see my enemies humbled! I swear it.*

"So far we have held both the Gatineau Habitats and the IronForge Shipyards. I do not know for how much longer."

"He knows our main deployments." *I have given him too much information,* she thought bitterly. "Surely we can use the information he has given us to some advantage?"

"I don't know how accurate it is," Lucien admitted.

"Find out. You *do* have spies, yes?"

"Yes, my Lady." He paused. *The spy network was neglected during the war. You demanded that we use strength, more than finesse.* "As you are no doubt aware, communications are still haphazard." Too many relay satellites had been destroyed during the war—every House had targeted those of their neighbors indiscriminately. "Contact with Cadixia is still intermittent at best. Repair efforts are underway, but available resources are limited."

"Our warships are better used in fighting, not rebuilding the satellite network."

Lucien said nothing.

"I know that some messages are arriving. What other disasters do you have to report?"

"Simard is striking hard at our garrison near Arabay." The garrison was protecting a fuel refinery in orbit of the gas giant. "They are well aware of the refinery's importance to our House." It supplied nearly seventy-five per cent of the fuel necessary to keep the Fleet operational.

"What patrols are being used?"

"Five patrols have been committed by Simard, led by the flagship, *Glorious.*"

"The *Glorious* has thwarted my plans before."

"The *Wooden Duck* ambush chief among them." The *Duck* had cost Bouchard two cruisers, Lalonde three cruisers, and Karul a single cruiser before Simard defeated it.

"What do you know about the captain?"

Lucien gestured to an aide. "Lieutenant?"

The man nodded. "Jacques Simard is a cousin to the current Lord of the House. He had a fairly distinguished career, showing skill instead of relying on family name for his rank. If anything, he gone out of his way to avoid making use of family connections. He's had a fairly standard career of numerous patrols along the major shipping lanes, with a few skirmishes over newly located comets and asteroids. I know of his participation in no major battles." *Until recently, there were no major battles to participate in!* "The only rumor I have heard recently is that he has a relationship with a fighter pilot formerly of House LaLonde."

Yvonne was intrigued. "A relationship you say?" *Hmmm, possible blackmail? A prisoner we could take perhaps.* "What's her name?"

"*His* name is Devin Shaw."

"Disgusting," Yvonne sneered. "Only an inbred House like Simard would permit such perversity." *I would have had them both killed.*

Lucien was checking his own notes.

"I want the *Glorious* destroyed."

"My Lady?"

"Make its destruction a priority condition."

"As you wish. Maybe its loss will convince House Simard to scale back its operations."

"Yes, perhaps." *That is not my care at all*, she thought. *I will not allow those deviants to exist in* my *Freehold.*

* * *

"Graham patrol closing."

"I see it." Natalie Hales eyed the displays as the patrol passed the asteroid. "Break and attack!" she ordered. The *Fenris* and its escorts lifted away from the crater where they had been hiding. "Fire all weapons!"

The brigantine and its cruisers began a hasty turn, trying to pull away from the Thibeau warships. The longer-ranged weapons concentrated on the brigantine first.

"*Crimson Rage* destroyed."

"Continue firing." Natalie had no intention of allowing any other House to approach Bonavista. *General Thibeau has ordered a line be drawn and I will stand fast.* "Status?"

"Minor damage to the *Werewolf*," her aide announced. "Two Graham ships destroyed, one has surrendered." He paused. "*White Sands* is powering down its drives and weapons."

"Send a boarding crew to take command." She smiled. "We welcome the addition of another cruiser to our House Fleet."

"And the prisoners?"

"Execute them." Natalie gave the command in a light tone. "The other Houses are not taking our warriors prisoner any longer so we shall not burden ourselves either." *The new face of warfare.*

* * *

"We must make plans for a joint assault."

Bouchard eyed the other Lords. "With yourself at the helm, LaLonde?"

"If necessary."

"I would prefer to see a neutral body in command of any fleet."

"There is no neutral body, Simard."

"I know that."

Karul stalked towards the table. "As long as Thibeau remains in command of Bonavista, she can continue to rebuild her military forces. Right now, Bonavista is all that she still holds."

Marcel Chenier nodded calmly. "Between us, we have claimed and captured every holding House Thibeau once held. All that remains now is Bonavista itself."

"The planet is held securely. All the recent raids have failed."

"Indeed, Lord Graham. We are aware of your rather pathetic showing."

Graham stood taller. "My ships are selling themselves dearly. I do not see any of you risking your own ships in attempts to defeat the renegades."

"We are not fools," Simard pointed out. *Nor do we have anything to prove. Your alliance with her was a mistake that you hope does not doom your House alongside hers.* "A single patrol cannot hope to penetrate their current defenses."

"If anything, we have improved their chances for survival," Bouchard said. "By destroying their other holdings, they now are free to concentrate their full military strength around one world. We have many holdings to defend and thus we must dilute our own naval strength accordingly."

"We should combine our fleets and launch one single devastating strike into the heart of our foe. With one swift blow, we could end this war." Karul waited, but no one agreed with his proposal. *Fools,* he thought bitterly. *I am surrounded by short-sighted fools!*

"If we leave our holdings vulnerable," Jonathan LaLonde said, "then we are inviting attack from Thibeau, or from another House."

"She will be too busy defending to risk an attack!" Dennis snapped.

"So you will allow her to hide on Bonavista?"

"We will attack Bonavista, if we are provided with agreements that other Houses will not attack us in turn." Jonathan LaLonde looked around the room. "Suitable agreements must be reached."

"Forget these damned agreements!" Raymond Tessier shouted. "That bitch must be killed. Gather your fleets and shatter her defenses. Damn the cost, just make it happen!"

"Calm yourself," Bouchard ordered. "You forget your place."

"My place?" Raymond snarled. "I am a Lord of the Cadian Freeholds!"

"You have nothing left to your House but a few streets in the capitol."

Raymond glared at other silent nobles. His hand grasped at his sidearm, though he did not draw it from its holster. "You bastard." His face was white.

"Lord Tessier, you must remain calm." Dennis Simard frowned. "The lack of military resolve shown by your fellow Lords is no reason for unjust anger."

"No reason? Are you all mad or just stupid? That bitch destroyed my holdings. She murdered my grandfather and my family. I am the last of my line."

"She will be punished."

"I will not hold my breath, Karul." He turned on his heel and strode from the room, his gray cloak flapping behind him.

* * *

"Confirmation has just arrived, General. The last of our off-world holdings has fallen."

"Our House has nothing left?"

The officer shook his head. "I'm afraid not, General."

Lucien Thibeau sighed loudly. "All that saves us now is the lack of unity amongst the other Houses."

Yvonne turned to her uncle. "How can you talk of defeat?' she demanded. "What of our military strength?"

"We have massed the bulk of our remaining patrols around Bonavista, my Lady. Our numbers are limited in comparison with what the other Houses can muster. Should they mobilize in strength, we will fall." Lucien felt so old and tired now. "I have authorized some of our most distant patrols to remain mobile, to raid targets of opportunity as best they can."

"Too little, too late, I fear."

"We can only do what we can, Yvonne. We are merely Human."

"The future of the greatest of the Noble Houses is at stake, Uncle. In times such as these, we must be able to become more than Human."

The old general shook his head. "We have no other assets left to us. One world cannot stand against the rest of the system."

"It must."

"We have lost everything, Yvonne." He tried to keep his voice quiet, so as to not dismay the officers in the command center. "We have no tricks left to play."

"We still have the *Gauntlet*."

"It is not a miracle ship. It cannot win this war."

"I am not defeated yet!" she hissed. "Not every asset is lost to me."

Lucien eyed her.

1 Chapter Twenty-Six

"The siege continues."

"What did you expect?"

Jacques eyed the main displays. "Looks like every ship she has left is out there." Along with a fully operational shipyard, an orbital space station at each pole, and possibly thousand of fighters.

"I wonder if she has any mines."

"I hope not. Or else this assault will get even messier."

* * *

"Still no word from Bonavista."

I had not expected any, though I had dearly hoped to hear that this damned war was over. Anne-Marie Desroches sighed aloud. "Take us ahead, full speed." Her brigantine, *Desperation*, moved towards the asteroid cluster. "There it is." ACL-Epsilon-Three.

"We're being warned off."

"Let them broadcast their pitiful threats...we have nothing to lose." The other Houses were fighting a dirty war now...and she would play by their rules. "Target the dome."

"Getting a target lock now."

"We're being tracked by the surface defenses."

"Keep our fighters clear." She would not need them for this. *I will not waste my pilots. Not when they are completely unnecessary.* "Fire."

Missiles streaked from their launchers. Her brigantine mounted five launchers; each launcher carried thirty missiles in its magazine. It only required forty-five of those one hundred fifty missiles to breach the dome and devastate the LaLonde colony.

"All communications from the colony have ceased."

Anne-Marie closed her eyes for a long moment as her soul screamed. "Recall our fighters. Set course for ACK-Delta-Two."

"What about survivors?"

She shook her head. "They called for help as we approached. Let LaLonde waste resources in coming to their aid. If anyone has survived, they're his concern." Such was the nature of the war. "We have other targets to deal with."

"Aye, Captain."

"Send a transmission packet to Bonavista. Update General Thibeau on our grand *success*." She choked on the words.

* * *

"*For glory!*"

The comm-system crackled with signals.

"Multiple fighter squadrons closing from all sides, Captain."

Jacques Simard took a deep breath. "Prep the anti-fighter defenses."

"Yes, Captain."

"Stand by to defend the ship." He stared at the bridge displays. There were a lot of fighters closing—Thibeau was launching a major strike at the blockade fleet.

"Fighters entering weapons range."

"Open fire."

"Fighter squadrons requesting permission to engage."

Keep safe, Devin. "Permission granted."

* * *

"Forward!" Raymond Tessier shouted into his comm. "Let us show the others how a true House fights and dies." His augmented patrol was all that remained of his House's strength. The brigantine, recently renamed *Bloody Retribution*, led seven cruisers towards the waiting ranks of Thibeau ships.

"They are heading for the shipyard."

"Stop them." Yvonne knew she could not afford to lose that last functional shipyard. Although her planetary factories could build more *Stilettos* and *Daggers*, only the orbital shipyards could replace her warships.

Lucien nodded. "The defenses will hold." *They have no choice.*

Yvonne had forsaken her opulent palace quarters and throne room to remain in the cramp command center during the ongoing siege. She had even exchanged her gowns for a military-trimmed jumpsuit. "I will hold you too that promise, Uncle."

"We can only do our best, Yvonne."

"Planet-based squadrons are standing by for launch, General."

"Hold them in reserve. If the rest of the blockade fleet moves, we'll need all the fighters we've got to hold them off from the planet." *The shipyard will be lost...either in this battle or in the next. That is the only thing I can truly promise to her.*

"General, the shooting has started."

Natalie snarled as one her cruisers blew apart. "Target the flagship and destroy it." The Tessier ships were fighting like madmen. A dozen Tessier fighters weaved through defensive fire to unleash missile salvoes into another one of her cruisers; only half of them survived the attempt.

Raymond didn't even feel pain. He knew that he should feel *something*—the *Retribution* had taken a fierce hit from a cruiser it had subsequently destroyed—from the metal shards that were impaling him. "Forward, press on!" he gasped.

The shipyard was just ahead. Hastily installed point defense guns were firing at the tattered remnants of his fighter squadrons. *Stilettos* traded shots with Thibeau fighters, while two squadrons of *Daggers* dove towards the orbital works.

"*Vengeance* destroyed!" an officer shouted. "*Just Desserts* is crippled."

Leaving only the *Avenger* to accompany *Bloody Retribution* on the final assault. The rest of his fleet had been destroyed. "So dies my House," he muttered. "Full speed to the engines!"

"We're not stopping them all!"

"Keep trying!" Natalie was amazed. That handful of ships had destroyed twice their number, and damaged just as many more and still the ships were advancing. *Even my ship has been hurt.* "How can Tessier still be fighting?" His flagship was a wreck, most of its weapons destroyed, the hull breached, and secondary explosions erupting outwards every few seconds, yet still it struggled.

"Shipyard defenses are reporting heavy damage from the fighters."

"Send them additional fighters." If she had any to spare.

"We've destroyed the last cruiser."

"Now hit the brigantine." It was getting much too close to the shipyards.

"Firing now."

How could he have survived this long? she wondered. *His ship is a wreck!* Yet it was still firing on the Yards. "Hit it again!"

"We're trying."

"It's on a collision course!" She stared numbly at the screen. "Do something!" she screamed.

* * *

"Thibeau has fallen back to near-orbit."

"Since the loss of their shipyards, they won't be too eager to keep fighting out there." Every lost ship would hurt them...they could not be replaced.

"Tessier sold his life dearly."

"We owe him." Karul knew those words were not enough, but at the moment, they were all that he had to offer.

"Fighter patrols are still strong."

"They keep building more...but even Thibeau can't keep finding replacement pilots. She must be getting near the end of her resources."

* * *

Lucien watched as a patrol died in desperate battle against three-to-one odds. "This is not battle, but slaughter." Yet what choice did he have? "Fight on," he ordered over the comm. "We will not falter in the final defense of our homes!"

Yvonne watched duly as icons representing her forces darkened. Granted, enemy ships were dying out there, but they had so many more than she did. They had started with more and most of their ships were not depleted and battered after so many previous fights.

"My Lady?"

"Keep fighting, Uncle," she told him, her voice like iron. "We will do what we can to hold this world." Or make the final battle so costly that the winning Houses would lament their victory for decades to come.

1 Chapter Twenty-Seven

"We have entered firing range on the planet. A few salvoes of missiles will end resistance."

"I will not condone a mass slaughter of innocents."

Karul sighed. *Maintaining a peace will be more difficult than winning the war,* he thought grimly. *With the taste of blood, will the other Houses accept anything less than genocide of Thibeau?* And did he want that House to survive? *They are tainted with blood...and their blood stains our hands as well.* It was not a choice he relished.

* * *

"The offer to surrender still stands, my Lady."

"I know. I refuse it." Yvonne stood defiantly in her command center. She knew that the eyes of her world were upon her. *I will not falter in the final moments of my rule!* "If any of the other Houses wish to take this world for themselves, then I welcome their attempts." She was resolved, a true Lady from the ancient legends. She would set an example for her soldiers.

"My Lady, you cannot do this."

"I can." She had found time to have her hair elegantly coiffed and her gown was exquisite. "I rule this House."

Lucien nodded. "True, Yvonne, but we have lost our navy. This House is weakened."

"We have many fighters."

"Not enough to fend off a full-scale invasion. Nor will the surface defenses be able to shoot down more than a handful of invading shuttles."

"Coward."

"I can defend the capitol for some time, but against those odds...."

"You suggest that we need a miracle?" Yvonne scoffed.

"We are beyond even a miracle."

"Uncle, I will not have you speak like that to me."

Lucien looked at her coldly. "I speak my mind, Yvonne. If you wish me removed from your presence then you may do so."

She considered banishing him, but then sighed. *He is the finest military mind remaining to this House. I cannot squander him...not when I need him alive if I am to have any hope of preserving some of my holdings.* "What do you suggest then?" she asked.

"Negotiate."

"*Negotiate?*"

"Surely we can come to some understanding at last. I do not believe the other Lords will wish to see this House utterly destroyed." Even with that fool announcement from the start of the war. "Bargain with them—with Karul. Give up a few of your perks and salvage what you can from this disaster. It is our only hope."

"What can I offer?" she asked. "The others have taken all of my other holdings. They've destroyed our military infrastructure. We are left with just Bonavista."

"Offer them whatever you have to. You have no choice."

"I cannot do this."

"You have no choice. For the good of our House, you must."

"No." Yvonne shook her head. "I will not surrender!"

Lucien Thibeau looked at her coldly. "Then I will." His voice was bitter.

* * *

Yvonne stormed along one of the corridors. "Betrayed!" she hissed. "By my own uncle." Two of her guards followed her. *At least I can trust them,* she thought bitterly.

"My Lady?"

Stopping in mid-step, Yvonne turned. "Yes?" she asked, as her gown fell still around her slender figure.

"Captain Neil Latimer, at your service."

"Yes, Captain?" Her eyes skimmed his uniform, noting the insignia on his shoulder. "Shouldn't you be with your ship?"

"The *Evening Breeze* is not a warship, my Lady. It's just a courier."

She nodded, recognizing the name. "A freighter."

"A freighter all-but-ignored by the warships fighting beyond orbit." Neil kept his voice calm. "A freighter with extra speed and some fancy ecm systems. The *Breeze* can slip through unsuspecting enemy patrols before they know we're there."

Yvonne smiled as she studied his face. "A freighter with room for a few passengers?"

"Yes, my Lady."

"You have a destination in mind?"

"Starbase Hidden Hope."

Her eyes narrowed. "One of my father's legacies."

"Yes, my lady."

"Take me to your ship, Captain. We have a date with destiny." She smiled, feeling a weight lift from her shoulders. "We will still have a chance for greatness! This House will yet survive."

Neil nodded. "And what of the General?"

"Leave him to his negotiations," she scoffed. "At best, they will distract the others while we escape."

"My freighter is this way." He gestured.

* * *

"The planet's defenders are still fighting."

Space around the planet was crowded with fighters and warships trading missile volleys and laser beams.

"I hope it doesn't come to orbital bombardment. I'd like to think that we will continue to hold the moral high ground in this butchery."

Jacques chuckled. "Devin, you are an idealist."

Devin shrugged.

"I, for one, am hoping that the other Lords don't forget themselves and start firing on each other." The inter-House alliance would not likely last for much longer. *It's a miracle it's lasted this long.*

"Captain, there's a ship breaking orbit."

"ID it."

"A freighter. Transponder reads *Evening Breeze*."

"It's just a civilian ship. Let it go."

"No heart to blast it?"

"No." Jacques shook his head. "Other freighters have fled...they're of no importance. Just carrying desperate refugees away before the fighting spills onto the surface."

"Broadcast from the planet's surface...Yvonne Thibeau is calling on her loyal followers to fight to the last breath. Slaughter those who would challenge the destiny of House Thibeau."

"Rubbish. Yvonne abandoned the rights and privileges of nobility by her orders to bombard colonies."

"The broadcast has ceased."

"*Jeweled Gauntlet* is firing on a Chernier patrol."

A bright flash lit one monitor.

"It's covering that freighter."

"Why?"

"Because it's a civilian?"

"Or because it carries someone important." Devin looked at his lover. "*Yvonne?*"

"Just like a rat...fleeing her doomed home." Jacques raised his voice. "Set a course for the *Breeze*. Maximum thrust."

"Aye, Captain."

"Order the rest of our patrol to engage the *Gauntlet*."

"Yes, Sir."

"I should be out there." Devin chewed at his inner lip. "My place is out in a fighter."

"You're not leaving my side."

1 Chapter Twenty-Eight

"Hidden Hope is just ahead, my Lady."

"Any sign of our pursuers?"

"Not yet."

"I hate to tell you this, Captain."

"Yes, Mitchell?" Neil asked.

"The sensors have been glitching. The new ECM system might be interfering with them."

"*Might* be?"

"I think that it is."

"Damn it! Why didn't you tell me that sooner?"

"I wasn't sure. I'm still not."

Neil muttered a few more curses. "My Lady, we should change course."

"No. We've been flying here at a pretty direct course, yes? They will know that we have a station or base out here."

"We're going to lead them to Hidden Hope."

"Yes, but luckily we have a secret strength."

"Which is?"

"Another star ship." Yvonne smiled at Neil. "Hidden Hope has been a research station for years. Most of the best and brightest minds in our House have been gathered there studying the *Gauntlet* and refurbishing a second ship. Major Sullivan can destroy the Simard ship pursuing us, and then we will evacuate Hidden Hope."

"In one ship?" Neil's eyes widened. "Does it have a working star-drive?"

"No, sadly. But it does have a fully functional cryo-stasis system. We will be able to depart from this star system at a high rate of sub-light and awaken in another star system. My House will rise again." She allowed the raw determination in her voice to carry across the bridge.

"We will rebuild our House on a new world. We will rediscover the secrets of our ancestors and return to Cadixia as conquerors!"

* * *

"It looks like a space station."

"Full alert."

"Warships detected. Multiple fighter squadrons incoming."

"All crew to battle stations." Jacques frowned. *Who knew she had so many assets left to her!* "This is going to be nasty."

"I'll be commanding the fighter strike."

"Be safe, Devin."

"I will." *As safe as can be.* He hurried from the bridge.

"Give me a reading on those ships. Identify them!" After so many centuries of war, active warships were tracked and identified fairly easily. Knowing a ship's history was an important part of battle.

* * *

"As per the terms of the Ceasefire, Lucien Thibeau has stepped down from the position of acting-Lord of House Thibeau and martial law remains in force. Yvonne Thibeau remains in hiding, though rumors abound that she fled Bonavisita prior to the surrender."

Yvonne listened to the report with half an ear. "Is the Simard force still closing?"

"Yes, my Lady." Sullivan gestured. "Our defenses will do their best."

"Destroy those ships and victory will still be ours. Destroy those ships and we can still escape."

"Buy time for the evacuation?"

"Yes."

"Lucien Thibeau is stepping through the entrance way now. He's waving to the citizens. The capitol city is quiet; a stunned mood seems to be prevalent. No doubt the citizens wonder what punishment will be exacted by the victorious Noble Coalition."

"Our fighters are being cut to pieces."

"I can see that, Major."

Devin flipped his fighter end-over-end and fired a missile at one of the pursuing *Stilettos*. The Thibeau fighter exploded.

"Another squadron is massing, Flight Commander."

"I see it, Jade-Two." Devin frowned. "All Jades, form up on me."

"There's a ship in that docking bay."

More of a shipyard than a docking bay, Jacques thought. "Is it another warship?" *We can't take on a second* Jeweled Gauntlet.

"I don't think so. Minimal power readings right now."

"Weapons range of the base in five seconds."

"All guns are cleared to fire on the base at will."

"Copy that."

"Send in our remaining fighters."

Devin felt his fighter lurch as a laser burned through his wing. "Give me some cover fire!" he snapped into the comm. "The station is still active."

"Copy that, Jade-Leader."

"Lucien is raising his hand to the crowd."

"Cripple that *Broadsword*. Why is that so difficult?"

"It's fighting well. We're not trained warriors, my Lady. We sat out the war. A handful of raids are scarcely sufficient to keep us at fighting trim. That Simard ship has been serving in active combat for almost a year."

"What was that? A gunshot? Ladies and gentlemen, General Thibeau is down! I think he's been shot!"

Starbase Hidden Hope shook as missiles detonated against its outer hull.

Yvonne stood with a defiant snarl on her face. "It ends like this?" she shouted over the wail of alarms. "My House will live on!"

* * *

"The war is over."

"Is it?" Devin asked.

"Yvonne is dead. This time there is no doubt." The Starbase and the unidentified ship docked with it were both rubble now. "Bonavista is in chaos with the occupation."

"Read the reports, Jacques. The entire Thibeau family is dead! Murdered. Assassinated if you prefer that term instead. Revenge by the other Houses."

"The House violated the rules of warfare."

"And it paid the ultimate price." Every asset had been claimed by another House. Its fleet was destroyed. Its warriors were dead. Its civilians had been absorbed into other Houses. "Will we strike their name from our history texts?"

"No, I think we will remember them for their crimes."

Devin shook his head. "This was not a battle of honor...it was a bloody massacre."

"Maybe we needed this slaughter."

Devin stared at his lover. "What? How can you say that?"

"Maybe this bloodshed will change the way the Houses interact. Maybe this will be the last of the Resource Wars." Jacques put his arms around Devin's shoulders. "Maybe the Freeholds will finally have peace." He paused, then smiled. "The same kind of peace I feel when I am with you."

Devin smiled. "I love you."

"I love you too."

"Let's head home."

Connect with Me Online:

Smashwords: http://www.smashwords.com/profile/view/MattKirkby

Follow on Twitter—https://twitter.com/talonspiritcat

Facebook: http://facebook.com/MattKirkby

Also by Matt Kirkby

A Novel of Lovecraftian Horror
The Death of Hope

Stories Of Feudal Japan
With Honour Veiled

The Empyrean Republic
Empress of All The Stars

Standalone
A Wyrm In the Heart
Cthonian Dragons
Forlorn Gambit
Reap What Has Been Sown
The Horror From The Sea
Vector Of Infection

About the Author

Born and raised in small-town Ontario, Matt Kirkby is a romantic dreamer who specializes in writing tales of high fantasy and pulp-style science fiction and space operas. He draws his inspiration from all diverse sources and ideas: Science Fiction, Fantasy, Gothic Horror, Pastoral Nature. He started his writing career submitting fan fiction for numerous Star Wars and TransFormers fanzines, but has since moved on to writing professionally. He published his first novel, A Wyrm In The Heart in 2004. He lives a double life, writing classy sci-fi and fantasy for fun under his own name, and penning gay erotica under the pen name of Frank Sol. When not writing, Matt spends his time helping his partner with his hand-crafted rocking chair business -- www.OffYourRocker.ca -- and trying to maintain some control over his cat. He still thinks that no gift is better than a new book.

www.ingramcontent.com/pod-product-compliance
Lightning Source LLC
Chambersburg PA
CBHW022001150726

47990CB00002B/543